Dear Romance Reader,

Welcome to a world of breathtaking passion and never-ending romance.
Welcome to *Precious Gem Romances*.

It is our pleasure to present *Precious Gem Romances*, a wonderful new line of romance books by some of America's best-loved authors. Let these thrilling historical and contemporary romances sweep you away to far-off times and places in stories that will dazzle your senses and melt your heart.

Sparkling with joy, laughter, and love, each *Precious Gem Romance* glows with all the passion and excitement you expect from the very best in romance. Offered at a great affordable price, these books are an irresistible value—and an essential addition to your romance collection. Tender love stories you will want to read again and again, *Precious Gem Romances* are books you will treasure forever.

Look for fabulous new *Precious Gem Romances* each month—available only at Wal★Mart.

Kate Duffy
Editorial Director

JANE-I'M-STILL-SINGLE-JONES

Joan Reeves

ZEBRA BOOKS
Kensington Publishing Corp.

http://www.zebrabooks.com

ZEBRA BOOKS are published by

Kensington Publishing Corp.
850 Third Avenue
New York, NY 10022

First Printing: August, 2000
10 9 8 7 6 5 4 3 2 1

Printed in the United States of America

You and I together were probably responsible for every gray hair in our parents' heads. From adopting orphaned opossums to burning down the outhouse, we did it all! Somehow, they—and we—survived and have a heck of a lot of funny stories to tell now!

This is for you, Vernon Lafayette Ainsworth, my partner in crime, my first best friend, and my big brother.

And, as always, for L.A.R. Thanks for the memories!

One

Jane Jones stared at the plastic-encased name tag in her right hand. No way would she wear it. She wasn't some boy-crazy teenager. Or a desperate woman on the make. She was a successful businesswoman. She'd even been called one of "the new sophisticates" in a *New York Times* column. But did that matter in Vernon, Louisiana? Heck, no!

So what if she still wasn't married? It shouldn't matter to anyone—with the possible exception of her mother—that she was still flying solo through life. Jane's eyes narrowed. Which of her former classmates was responsible for this embarrassment?

"Jane Louise Jones! Quit staring at that name badge as if it were going to bite you and put it on."

Jane's focus shifted from the detestable piece of plastic to the woman who'd handed her the reunion packet. Her eyes widened in dismay. Belatedly, she recognized her high school nemesis presiding at the reception table. Of all people, why did it have to be Earleen Mushmak?

The woman's thin lips stretched in a grimace that almost resembled a smile. "Welcome to your ten-year high school reunion, Jane Louise." She cocked her head to the side as if in deep thought. Then she said, "That's very daring of you to wear scarlet, dear. Most redheads would think better of it."

Some high school traumas never die, Jane thought. This one looked as if she hadn't aged a day.

"Thank you, Miss Mushmak," Jane murmured, trying hard to remember that she was a grown woman, not some high school kid unused to dealing with difficult people.

Often, Jane joked with her family about traveling through a time warp to get from New York to her sleepy hometown tucked away in the rolling hills of north Louisiana. But, looking at the woman who had taught at the local high school since before Jane was born, she half believed it was true.

Her former teacher hadn't changed a bit—unfortunately. The years appeared to have had no softening effect on the woman who struck fear into the heart of every freshman entering Vernon High School. Same straggly bun. Same steel-rimmed granny glasses. Same piercing gray eyes that made you believe she had x-ray vision.

The bossy old maid had never liked her, Jane thought resentfully, nor any of her other students—except one. And thinking about *him* only increased Jane's ire.

She fingered the name tag and took a deep breath. She'd laugh and toss it back on the table. They could darn well give her a blank one. Then she'd write her own inscription next to her name.

"Did you hear me, Jane Louise?" Miss Mushmak

demanded, pushing her glasses down on her nose and peering over them.

The double moniker rubbed Jane the wrong way. In New York, she was J. L. Jones, owner of JLJ Design. Here, she was plain Jane Louise.

"Jane Louise?" Miss Mushmak repeated, with more snap to her tone this time. The woman, who'd tried her best to hammer math into Jane's decidedly un-mathematical brain from her freshman to her senior years, stared at her just as she'd done back in high school.

Jane reacted like the new sophisticate she was. She squirmed and replied meekly, "Yes, Miss Mushmak."

"Good. Don't dawdle. Step aside to pin on your name tag."

"Yes, Miss Mushmak." She'd step aside, but she darn well wasn't going to wear the name tag.

Coward, she scolded herself, even as she moved away from the reception table. Ten years after graduation, and she was still terrified of the teacher. It made no sense. What could Miss Mushmak do now? Flunk her again?

Her gesture of defiance might be small, but it lifted her spirits. Looking around, she saw refreshments set up on gold paper-covered tables in the center of the large room that served as cafeteria and auditorium for the old school.

Maybe some caffeine would short-circuit the tension headache that threatened at the base of her neck, she thought. Jane had taken only a few steps when someone grabbed her arm and spun her around.

"Amber!" Jane's scowl changed to a grin. She

grabbed her best friend from high school and hugged her. Amber squealed and giggled.

Even at twenty-eight, Amber Hicks—Amber Hicks Chalmers, Jane mentally corrected—couldn't control her excitement. Same old Amber, Jane thought fondly, stepping back to look at her friend.

"Oh, Janie, I can't believe you really came." Amber jumped up and down like a child of six rather than a mother of a six-year-old. She'd been doing that crazy little jig since she and Jane had played together in kindergarten.

"What do you mean? You twisted my arm, begged, pleaded, and then sicced the town on me. It's bad enough to have my parents badger me, but the Ladies Bridge Club, too? With all that, how could I possibly miss this momentous occasion?"

"Hey, don't give me that blasé New York attitude. This is our ten year reunion! Aren't you excited?"

"Not as much as you are."

"It'll be fun. You won't be sorry you came," Amber vowed.

Jane sighed. "I'm already sorry. To think I gave up the first weekend in June to come here and be humiliated."

"What do you mean humiliated?" Amber frowned.

Jane held up the name tag. "Look at this."

"What's wrong with it?" Amber looked affronted. "I spent a lot of time designing those."

"Oh, Amber. Don't tell me you're responsible for this. How could you do this to me?" Jane shook her head in dismay. "Set up by my best friend!"

"Well, you said you lacked a love life. I thought this would help."

"I said I had a lackluster love life," Jane corrected. "There's a difference." She rolled her shoulders to loosen the tension. "Now I really need some caffeine and sugar. You just changed the status of my headache from passive to active."

"What are you complaining about?" Amber grabbed the pin from Jane's hand and, ignoring her protests, fastened it to the right lapel of her red linen blazer. "There."

Amber stepped back and studied the name tag. "I was worried the print wasn't large enough to easily read, but it's okay."

Jane looked down at her chest. "You can probably read it from Mars," she muttered. "Without a telescope."

"Quit grumbling. Come on." Amber took her arm and guided her to the refreshments. "Your blood sugar must be low. You always get cranky when you're hungry."

"I'm not cranky," Jane protested. Nevertheless, she picked up a gold paper plate and a black napkin. There must be something symbolic in this, she decided, as she followed Amber around the table. She'd been following Amber's lead since they were kids. Amber was the impulsive adventurer who leaped right into the middle of life, wanting to be surprised, while Jane was the careful analyst who always looked before leaping. Well, almost always, Jane mentally amended.

"You've got to try these cookies. I made them from Aunt Judy's recipe." Amber placed two golden brown mounds studded with chunks of pecan, chocolate, and raisins on Jane's plate.

Jane shook her head in amazement. "I've seen you in the kitchen, but I still can't get used to the idea that you're a domestic goddess." Jane bit into a cookie. She rolled her eyes and moaned in delight. "No wonder Steve married you a week after he met you."

"I didn't know how to boil water when I met Steve. Believe me, that was not what captured my husband." Amber smiled archly.

"Great sex, huh?" Jane took another bite.

"Let's just say that women who think the way to a man's heart is through his stomach don't know much about anatomy."

That comment got a laugh from Jane. "Amber, you're terrible."

"Nope. I'm incorrigibly honest."

"Whatever you say." Jane finished the cookie. "These are fantastic. How can you stay so thin when you bake?"

"Hey, you try running after a six-year-old bundle of energy masquerading as a boy. You'd be skinny too. Not that you're fat," Amber added with a grin. "Go grab a couple of chairs before they're all taken, and I'll get us two coffees."

"Anyone ever tell you that you're bossier than ever?"

"Yep. My husband—practically every day. Still drink your coffee black?" At Jane's nod, she shooed her with both hands. "Go save our seats."

Jane complied. The reunion was a great excuse to catch up with Amber. Some of Jane's tension eased, leaving her feeling more relaxed than since she'd arrived. Maybe the weekend wouldn't be so bad after all.

On the other side of the room, folding chairs had been set up in semicircular rows beneath the old-fashioned high windows.

"It's safe to say that there's plenty of chairs to go around," Jane said over her shoulder. "The reunion hasn't exactly drawn a crowd."

"Hey, this is just registration." Amber came up behind her. "Wait until later. Nearly everyone responded to the seventy invitations we mailed." She handed Jane a white Styrofoam cup.

"You're kidding." Jane accepted the steaming coffee. "You told me that not everyone would attend the reunion." That had been the deciding factor in her own acceptance of the invitation. Before she could question Amber further, her friend jumped up.

Setting her plate and cup on the chair next to her, Amber said, "Let me get you some more cookies."

"I haven't finished these," Jane protested, but Amber was already rushing away. Jane watched as her friend seemed to take an inordinate amount of time to select a few cookies. She frowned. What was going on here? When Amber returned, Jane asked again about the reunion attendance.

"Oh, uh, well, I guess I did say the attendance would be light," Amber stammered. "But at the last minute, I, that is, the reunion committee, received several calls. Apparently, a lot of people changed their mind." She stuffed a cookie nearly whole into her mouth.

"Like who?" Jane asked, feeling the muscles at the back of her neck clench tighter.

Amber chewed and pointed at her mouth, earning another frown from Jane. Surely Amber would have told her if *he* had decided to come. After all, he was the most famous alumnus their small high school could boast. He'd gone into the world and made millions, or at least that's what the town gossips maintained. Jane had never seen his name in the news or in the papers. Not that she had looked—much. Of course, that didn't mean anything. There were more wealthy men and women who weren't household names than the other way around.

When Amber had swallowed, Jane persisted. "Like who?"

"Oh, just people. You know, those of us who stayed in town will be here with spouses in tow. Though I hope no one brings their kids. My mom is taking little Stevie to the lake for the weekend."

Amber shrugged and concluded weakly, "That's all I meant by a good turnout. Reunions are always popular. Most kids who deserted their hometown for the bright lights of the big city like the chance to reconnect with high school friends."

Jane broke a cookie in half and absently crumbled it as she studied her friend. Amber's explanation was a little too pat.

"You know how it is in a small town." Amber laughed. "Anything out of the ordinary draws a crowd. This is high class entertainment for us local yokels." Amber added a packet of artificial sweetener and a tiny tub of cream to her coffee, then stirred with a plastic spoon. "Even Steve is looking forward to coming," she rattled on, "and you know what he thinks about the social life here."

"Well, Steve was raised in the mean streets of Beverly Hills. I guess he finds small town entertainment a bit tame," Jane said, careful not to crack a smile.

"Mean streets?" Amber giggled. "I'll have to tell that to Steve. And it wasn't Beverly Hills."

Jane resolved not to say any more about the whole matter. She could always steal quietly away if *he* showed up.

"You should have seen Steve's ten-year reunion a couple of years ago. I swear, I think everyone including husbands, wives, and children showed up. We ran out of food after the first hour, when I thought there was enough to feed an army."

"Sounds as if his school was a lot bigger than ours."

"There were about six hundred in his graduating class."

"That's a far cry from our seventy-three." Jane suspected Amber was keeping something from her, but she was too tired to engage in a cross-examination.

"I could teach you how to make these cookies," Amber offered. "They're easy."

"You're really into this domestic thing, aren't you?" Jane stared a bit wistfully at her friend, wondering what it was like to be a stay-at-home mom, baking cookies and making name tags for some committee or other.

"Call me old-fashioned, but I love my life. Sometimes, though, I do wonder what it would be like to live yours. It seems so exciting, living in the Big Apple.

Who would ever have thought that you'd become a famous textile designer? That's amazing."

"It's not that big a deal. And I don't think you could call me famous. No one knows who I am except for those in the industry." Jane shrugged. "My life's okay, I guess."

Only to Amber would she confess her growing dissatisfaction. Jane had fought so hard for her independence that she didn't want to admit to anyone that her life wasn't perfect.

"When I first went to art school in New York, I thrived on the excitement of the city. It was new and completely different from anything I'd ever known. There was so much to see and do and learn that I didn't have time to think about"—Jane's gaze flitted away—"about anything else. But now?" Her voice cracked. "I'll tell you something if you promise not to tell anyone else."

Amber made a crossing motion over her heart and a zipping motion over her lips.

"Lately, I find myself thinking about a home and children. And when I do, I don't visualize raising a child in my loft in the city. I think of my house here— the tree house in the backyard and the swing on the front porch. I never knew how much I loved this place until I left."

Amber nodded. "I can understand your wanting the traditional family, but you didn't say anything about a husband. Don't you imagine a man as the father of those children?"

Jane's shoulders drooped. "That's the trouble. I can't see any man in that picture."

Well, that wasn't precisely true. She did see one man's face, but that was the result of a long-ago case of puppy love. *He* would never do—even if she knew where he was.

"So you've begun to think about something other than your career?" Amber grinned. "I must say, better late than never."

"Fat lot of good it does me," Jane grumbled. "I'm beginning to wonder if I'll end up alone. Statistics aren't exactly in my favor." She dropped the cookie she held onto the plate. Her appetite had disappeared.

"I try to convince my mother and grandmother that I'm perfectly happy with my life, but I guess I'm not or I wouldn't be confessing my deep dark secret to you." Jane scowled. "And if you breathe a word of this, I'll never speak to you again."

"I won't tell anyone. Go ahead and pretend to be Ms. Single Success to your heart's content. Now, as for thinking there are no men available, don't be ridiculous. There's a wonderful guy out there just waiting for you," Amber said loyally.

Jane smiled. "Thanks, you're a pal. But in another forty years, I might be an old maid like Earleen Mushmak, dried up and as sour as one of Granny's homemade pickles."

Amber choked on her coffee. "Please. Don't say things like that when I have a full mouth."

"You don't think that's a possibility?"

"Somehow, Janie, I can't picture those short auburn curls as a straggly gray bun. And I bet you wouldn't be caught dead in an ankle-length, flowered dress or no-nonsense shoes."

"Well, that part is certainly true." Jane smoothed her hands down the short red skirt. She looked at her feet arched by the red high heel sandals.

"You're not even thirty yet. You've got plenty of time to find the man of your dreams," Amber said. "All it takes is a chance encounter." She lifted her coffee cup in a salute. "Here's to good luck."

"I'll drink to that," Jane said, clicking her cup to Amber's. The first swallow of coffee reminded her that people in Louisiana tended to make their coffee rather strong. This batch was stout enough to keep Sleeping Beauty awake despite the wicked witch's curse.

"Maybe you'll get lucky this weekend."

"I don't think that's a possibility." Jane laughed at the idea. "I can't think of any of my former class mates who could be called the man of my dreams."

"Are you sure about that?" Amber asked, opening her eyes wide. "Wasn't there a certain boy?"

Jane's suspicions rose anew. She'd shared practically everything with Amber from the time they were toddlers—except that. *He* was her secret.

"I don't know what you mean," she said, hoping her fair skin wouldn't give her away with another blush.

"Well, just in case you do meet some wonderful guy, he'll be able to tell immediately that you're available, thanks to your specially designed name tag," Amber crowed.

Jane groaned. "Is that why I'm wearing this"—she

grabbed her lapel and shook it—"this embarrassment?"

"Hey, that's not embarrassing. That's a work of art. I even printed them in the school colors of black and gold. And let me tell you, it wasn't easy coming up with a one-liner to put on that many name tags!"

"Why didn't you just put my name on it and leave it at that? Or say I own my own design business. Anything but this."

"But that wouldn't have accomplished anything. Come on, be cool. This will be a fun weekend." Hands on hips, she said, "You're a businesswoman. You know the value of advertising."

"Is that what this thing on my chest is supposed to be? A walking ad? To sell me?" Jane squawked.

"Kind of. At least all the single guys will know you're available. You might renew an old friendship, and it could turn into something romantic."

"Sure. That makes sense. And we could date each other on the weekend. Right? We'd alternate dates in New York and dates here!"

"Don't be sarcastic, Janie. You don't know what will happen this weekend. It could be something totally surprising."

"Amber Chalmers, it's bad enough when my family gets on my case about not being married. As if an unmarried female of twenty-eight was somehow unnatural. Maybe it is in Louisiana, but not in New York."

"Since you just confessed your deep dark secret to me, it's too late for you to play the outraged feminist now," Amber said dryly.

"I was suffering from cookie poisoning earlier," Jane grumbled. "I am an outraged feminist."

Amber's eyes narrowed. "You can try that Gloria Steinem speech on your mother and granny, but it won't wash with me, and I bet it goes in their right ear and out their left."

"You're right. But at least it's a good speech. If I say it enough times, maybe I'll begin to believe it. But if you say otherwise, I'll—I'll tell Steve how you used to practice French kissing on your Cabbage Patch doll."

"Oh, that's low. You wouldn't!"

"Don't push me. I'm desperate." Jane sighed. "With both my sisters married and working, I have to listen to how the two of them balance marriage and a career. As if I'd ever been offered that opportunity."

"So if the younger sisters can do it, so can you?" Amber asked.

"Yeah. That's about the size of it, but the older I get, the harder it is to find a good prospect."

"Hey, I know you've had relationships, " Amber said.

"I can count my so-called serious relationships on my index fingers." She'd come close, but something always held her back—kept her aloof from the men who sought to woo her. She could honestly say there'd never been a serious romance in her entire life—unless you counted her secret fling in high school. And she didn't count that. She tried not to even think about it. Except sometimes. Late at night. That's when *he* sneaked into her dreams.

"Jane Louise! You don't look a day older," a woman squealed, interrupting her solemn thoughts.

Jane certainly hoped she looked different. After all, she'd paid a small fortune for the hair style she currently had, not to mention the red linen suit, royal blue silk tank, and red patent shoes. She smiled uncertainly at the woman. She couldn't place her. The voice was familiar, but she didn't recognize the spiky blond hair and the expensive tanned, toned body, nor the exquisitely made-up face.

"It's me—Felicia Banks!"

Jane's mouth dropped. "Felicia?" This woman didn't look anything like her chubby brunette friend from high school. She and Amber echoed in unison, "Felicia Banks?"

"Of course, who else?" The woman grabbed her and hugged her within an inch of her life.

Jane gasped for breath. "My goodness but you're strong. I mean, you look great." Amber chimed in on that compliment.

"Toned, tight, and terrific," Jane read Felicia's name tag. "Good tag. It certainly fits."

Felicia read Jane's and burst into laughter. "Yours is too funny."

"Yeah. Too funny." Jane gave Amber a sour look.

"Felicia, what on earth happened to you?" Amber asked. "I mean, I haven't seen you since graduation. You look terrific. How did it happen?"

Felicia laughed, then proudly told them about her chain of fitness salons in Texas.

The three women gave brief versions of the past ten years. Jane found herself enjoying the conversation.

"So you're a hot-shot designer," Felicia said. "I'm

impressed. But, how on earth do you stand it in New York?"

"I like it there," Jane said. For several minutes, she defended her adopted city. "I could well ask how Amber stands it in Vernon. Or you, Felicia, in Houston. That's not exactly a small village. Isn't it the third or fourth largest city in the United States now?"

"The fourth," Felicia said.

"It's all in what you get used to," Jane summed up.

"Well, we might both be-big city girls now, but,"— she pointed at Jane's name tag—"I see we've both come back to our hometown to go husband hunting."

"I am not husband hunting!" Jane protested. She was mortified. She'd known everyone would think the same thing when they read the stupid tag. "This was Amber's idea."

"Hey, if you're not looking for a man, that's fine with me. I only came because I'd heard that eight of the boys from our graduating class are single. And I'm hoping they're all going to be here."

Amber laughed. "Felicia, don't tell me you're still as boy-crazy as you were in high school?"

"Hey, I'm still the same simple girl. The only difference is that now I have the face and the body to compete with you cheerleader types," Felicia answered.

"I doubt that any of the boys from our graduating class would ever be asked to pose for the cover of a romance novel," Jane said, laughing. "Then or now."

"Yes, but I tend to believe that people improve with age. I mean, look at me." Felicia twirled. "By this age, girlfriends, men also will have made their mark in the world so the struggle years are out of the way. I can't wait to see the guys."

"You've really given this some thought," Amber said, sounding impressed.

"Sure have. I'm looking for Mr. Felicia Banks number three."

"Number three!" Amber looked stunned. "I think I'd give up if I were a two-time loser in matrimony." As soon as the words were out, she clapped her hand over her mouth. "I didn't mean that the way it sounded, Felicia."

"Hey, don't worry about it. And, no, you wouldn't give up either," Felicia replied, not seeming offended at all by Amber's tactless remark. "I don't mind telling you my number-one contender for number three will be here this weekend."

"Who might that be?" Jane asked, amused by her friend's refreshing honesty.

"Why, who else but the richest man that ever hailed from Vernon, Louisiana?" Felicia replied smugly.

Amber jumped to her feet. "Janie, I need to go to the restroom. Why don't you come with me?"

"Who do you mean?" Jane asked, alarmed.

"Let's go now, Janie." Amber tugged Jane's arm.

"My goodness, Jane Louise, haven't you heard? Morgan Sherwood's going to be here—along with his entourage, I expect."

Jane felt as if the breath had been knocked out of her body. She turned accusing eyes on Amber.

Him!

"Did I forget to tell you, Janie?" Amber asked, twisting her fingers in distress.

"Yes, as a matter of fact, you did forget." Jane tried to keep her voice calm. She'd make some kind of excuse and leave, she thought. No way would she spend three days—and nights—in the company of Morgan Sherwood! The thought made her feel faint.

Somewhere in the room, she heard something heavy slam to the floor. A muffled exclamation and hurried footsteps penetrated her shock, but she couldn't turn to see what the commotion was.

"I guess we don't have to flip a coin to see who gets Morgan then?" Felicia asked.

"Certainly not. You're welcome to the man," Jane said icily. She would die before she'd allow anyone to think she had ever been smitten with the class genius. "In fact, I hope his money makes up for his looks because he certainly wasn't much in high school. I doubt that's changed."

"Jane Louise!" Amber said sharply. "You shouldn't—"

"I shouldn't what? Speak the truth?" Jane's voice rose, unaware that the room had fallen silent.

Bent on making sure no one thought she was man-hunting, or less than happy with her life, as implied by the stupid name tag, she continued. "I'm not looking for a husband. I'm perfectly happy in my unmarried state, and I wish everyone in this town would realize that. I have the freedom to come and go as I please without answering to a man. And I support myself. I don't need a husband for that. So why would I want one? You can have the milk without buying the cow, if you get my drift. Men knew that for years before we women discovered that fact."

Felicia looked at her rather oddly. "So you don't think Morgan is a good catch?"

Jane forced a laugh. "I wasn't impressed with him ten years ago. Why should I change my mind just because he's got a few bucks in the bank?"

"Actually, that's ten million in stocks, bonds, precious metals, and bucks in the bank," a deep voice behind her corrected.

Jane whirled and came face to face with a dark-haired man who towered over her. His mouth stretched in a smile that revealed dazzling white teeth. A silly thought flitted through her stunned brain.

The better to eat you with, my dear.

Jane suppressed the hysterical giggle that bubbled upward. He wasn't the Big Bad Wolf, but she felt a lot like Little Red Riding Hood at the moment. She stared into his intensely blue eyes—eyes as unfathomable—and as cold, she realized—as the north Atlantic.

"Morgan!" Jane's voice was a whisper, yet, in the suddenly silent auditorium, it rang out. Two things about Morgan Sherwood hadn't changed—his voice and his eyes.

"Hello, Jane." His eyes looked intently into hers.

Make that three things that hadn't changed, she thought, with the way she felt when he said her name being the third. She shivered and remained silent.

His smile widened, but it wasn't really a smile, Jane thought dizzily. It was a smirk. A smug, macho smirk—aimed at her. He looked pointedly at her name tag.

"Jane-I'm-Still-Single-Jones," he read. "With a personality like yours, that's understandable."

Two

His remark hit her like a bucket of cold water in the face. Jane sputtered and came up fighting. "There is absolutely nothing wrong with my personality."

No one could hear her strident denial over the outburst of laughter. Jane blushed a red that rivaled the color of her suit. Then she made the mistake of looking at Morgan again. His smirk was even . . . smirkier!

She clamped her lips together. He'd be old and gray before she apologized for her less than flattering remarks. It wasn't her fault that he'd sneaked up and eavesdropped. She opened her mouth to tell him exactly what she thought, but Felicia took that moment to capture Morgan's attention. She literally shoved Jane aside in her haste to get to him.

"Well, I have a different opinion!" Felicia exclaimed, not even with so much as a blush. "Jump into Felicia's arms, Morgan the Multimillionaire. I'll be glad to catch you because I think you're absolutely hunk-alicious!" She grabbed Morgan and planted a kiss right on his mouth.

Jane felt her simmering anger explode. What made it even worse was that Morgan's eyes never left hers. She wouldn't give him the satisfaction of seeing her blink or look away. She stared unflinchingly into his eyes.

The corners of his eyes crinkled as if he were smiling, then he looked away. His eyes closed as he returned Felicia's kiss. Felicia's long scarlet fingernails trailed up through his dark brown hair.

Everyone whooped and cheered while Jane's blood pressure soared. She wanted to snatch Felicia's overly toned arms from him. When they came up for air, Morgan grinned at Felicia and tweaked one of the bleached blond spikes of hair.

"Nice to see you too, Felicia," he said.

To Jane's disgust, he didn't even seem winded from Felicia's exuberant welcome. Of course, he was six feet of rippling muscle. Make that tanned, rippling muscle, she thought, noting how his sun-bronzed features contrasted sharply with the starched white collar of his shirt. Quite a difference from high school. He'd been all wiry, lean muscles then. And what had happened to the pop bottle-thick glasses he'd worn? She'd only noticed his gorgeous eyes when he'd removed them before kissing her.

Jane clamped down on that traitorous thought. That way lay madness and sleepless nights.

She'd never admit it, but Felicia and Morgan looked good together, like a poster for a health club, or a swinging singles resort, she thought sourly. So he thought that was a kiss? She sniffed. What she wouldn't give to show Morgan Sherwood what she'd learned about kissing in the last ten years!

That thought rippled through her like a shock wave, and Jane felt her face heat again. What on earth was she thinking? She didn't want to kiss him. She hadn't even wanted to see him! She dared not look at Morgan for fear he would pick up on her insane thoughts.

Amber rescued her. "Come on, Janie." She linked arms with her. "I know just the drink to chase that big platter of foot-in-mouth."

Even as he exchanged comments with his former classmates, Morgan watched Jane leave. To a casual observer, his expression of amusement didn't alter, but to anyone who knew him well, a number that could be counted on one hand, he was visibly upset. It could be seen in the slight tightening at the corners of his lips, the minute narrowing of his eyes, and the way his smile didn't extend any farther than his lips. Friends and observant foes alike would have recognized Morgan Sherwood was in a snit.

"Morgan, is that big white limo yours?" someone called out.

Morgan heard someone answer, "Well, who else do you think it belongs to? The funeral home?"

Morgan had no interest in the talk that flowed around him. So Jane wasn't impressed ten years ago, and his hard-earned fortune wouldn't change her mind now. He clamped down on the anger and hurt. She couldn't have made it more obvious that she held him in disdain.

Somehow, over the years, he'd managed to convince himself that he hadn't given Jane a chance ten years ago. Ha! What a laugh. Good thing none of his business rivals knew how easily he could be suckered by a green-eyed redhead.

Worse, he'd had some insane idea that this weekend she'd fall into his arms. In his mind's eye, he had seen them rushing toward each other, like lovers in some slow-motion commercial. Well, he'd had part of the fantasy right—he'd just cast the wrong woman in the role of lover.

Morgan rolled his tongue around to see if it was still attached after Felicia's enthusiastic welcome. He'd have to make sure he wasn't trapped into kissing her again, he thought. His tongue probably couldn't sustain the trauma.

If Jane hadn't been watching, he'd have avoided Felicia's greedy mouth, but the look on Jane's face was worth a little discomfort. So why was he wondering how Jane's mouth would feel beneath his? Would her kisses excite him now as much as they had ten years ago?

Not that he cared, he hastily reminded himself. She'd used him in high school. He didn't plan to let her have another go at him, despite his foolish fantasies. He should never have come to this reunion. It was an exercise in futility. He already had the answer he needed so he might as well go.

Someone hollered, "Can I ride in your limo, Morgan? Just to show Bobbi Sue?"

"Me, too. Me too, please, Morgan?" an attractive woman with a *café au lait* complexion called out, her richly melodic voice rising above the others. That voice broke through his preoccupation and made his smile turn genuine. Little Verna Wright. Verna wasn't so little anymore, he noticed. She looked as if she'd actually grown a few inches, in addition to filling out in a most attractive way. She'd been like him—another round peg in a square hole.

Her voice was still the same—music to the ears. He wasn't surprised to see his friends turn to look at the person who possessed that voice. Even in high school, Verna's voice was like a combination of Aretha Franklin and Lena Horne—surprisingly rich coming from a pint-sized girl like her.

The knot of people around him grew unruly in their zeal to get close to him, pushing and shoving his people aside. He'd better do something before Berkley took over, he decided.

"Excuse me a moment, Felicia," Morgan said, prying her hands from his left arm.

Berkley, who usually posed as his driver, would be having a fit. He was probably salivating at the chance to use some of his Secret Service training to protect and defend. Poor Berkley. Guarding a businessman wasn't nearly as exciting as the White House detail he'd had before life had nearly done him in.

Morgan noted with surprise that Berkley's eyes weren't scanning the room as they usually did. Instead, his friend was staring with unguarded interest at Verna Wright. Interesting, Morgan thought. He'd never noticed Berkley show any interest in a woman since his fiancée had died two years ago.

The crowd grew more boisterous by the minute. Berkley's eyes snapped to Morgan. Seeing the fierce frown that appeared suddenly on his friend's face, Morgan jerked his head toward the steps leading up to the stage. If he didn't control matters, he'd find himself whisked away by his overzealous pal. Wryly, Morgan reflected on how a few million dollars had made him Mr. Popularity with his high school crowd.

He climbed the five steps to the stage. Pitching his voice loud enough to be heard over the murmur of the small crowd, he said, "It's great to see all of you too. I'd like you to meet some of my friends. Since they'll be staying in Vernon this weekend also, I ask that you offer them some good old-fashioned southern hospitality." He beckoned to the trio to approach. "Make way for them please."

The crowd split down the middle, allowing his three friends, who'd long since become more than employees, to join him. He grinned at the long-suffering looks on their faces. None of them had wanted to leave Los Angeles for what Penny called the boondocks, but he'd insisted. He'd told them they all deserved a weekend away, in the pastoral setting of small town America. In actuality, he'd needed the moral support of their friendship to confront the past and lay it to rest.

"This is my administrative assistant Penny Tranh. She knows where all the bodies are buried, so to speak." He'd met Penny when he'd gone back to Harvard to speak a few years ago. Her keen mind and dry humor had attracted his interest. Impulsively, he'd told her to look him up when she graduated, and she had.

Penny straightened her black suit jacket, rolled her eyes at him, and stuck out her tongue so that only he noticed as she walked up the steps to stand next to him. Morgan grinned. "She's single, guys. Spread the word."

"Like I want some slow-talking southern boy like you?" she hissed through smiling teeth.

"Hey, don't underestimate southern boys," Morgan said.

"And this gentleman—come on, Carlos, don't be shy. Carlos Dominguez is one of our management trainees. He's single too."

Carlos, though new to his staff, wasn't new to Morgan. He'd known Carlos since the kid had been in junior high. Morgan had been part of a volunteer program that matched businessmen as mentors to minority students. Carlos, a recent MBA graduate, had come a long way, and Morgan couldn't be more proud of him.

Carlos looked a bit uncomfortable, but he smiled gamely and waved as he stepped up. A sleepy southern town was as alien to the kid from Los Angeles as that city's *barrios* would be to the residents of Vernon.

"And this gentleman is Berkley. If you have any questions about the limo in front, he's the man to answer them. If you want a ride, don't ask me. Ask Berkley. It's his car."

"Thanks a lot," Berkley muttered to Morgan.

"No problem." Morgan grinned, not intimidated by Berkley's gruffness. He and Berkley had roomed together at Harvard and stayed close despite their different career paths. Berk was the only man Morgan trusted completely, and Morgan was the only man who could use Berk's given name without fear of retaliation.

Morgan leaned close to his friend's ear. "Play nice, Socrates, and I'll introduce you to her later."

Berkley's dark face split in a friendly grin as he faced the crowd and waved.

If nothing else came of this weekend, Morgan thought, he wouldn't regret coming because of the effect it was having on Berk. His friend had more expression in his eyes than he'd seen in months. Morgan suspected Berk's mourning was coming to an end.

"I'm sure we can arrange something for those who want to ride in a stretch limo," Berkley said, his frown transforming to a smile. "Just ask, and I'll see what I can do."

"Now if you'll excuse me, I think I'm going to get some of those delicious-looking refreshments," Morgan said.

The crowd ignored him and pushed to cluster around Berkley.

Morgan grinned. He'd suspected that the stretch limo might prove more of an attraction than his own person. Berk might not like it, but at least making him the center of attention took the pressure off Morgan.

"Now where were we?" Felicia asked, reclaiming his arm.

Morgan groaned inwardly but nodded and smiled at Felicia as she chattered on, though he couldn't have repeated one word the woman said. His thoughts drifted to Jane. Ten years was way too long to carry a torch for a woman who didn't know he was alive.

He felt like putting his fist through a wall. He could take over whole companies but couldn't seem to conquer his infatuation for that woman. But he planned to work on it from this moment on. No man in his right mind would want her. Jane Jones was full of her-self—just as conceited as she'd been in high school. He wasn't about to let her break his heart again.

Jane sank onto the bench at the school bus loading ramp. She was mortified that Morgan had walked in during her flamboyant monologue. Or she would be as soon as her brain finished cataloging the attributes of the new and improved version of Morgan Sher-wood. He looked so different. But he still had that special something that made her pulse throb, more's the pity.

"Felicia was right," Jane said.

"About what?" Amber asked, sitting down next to her.

"About men improving with age."

"Yep. If Morgan improved any more they'd have to arrest him for contributing to the indecency of fe-males."

"I don't think there's an actual law on the books regarding that," Jane said. Her fingers traced a heart some young lover had carved into the weather-worn cypress a few decades ago.

"Well, if there isn't, there should be," Amber said.

Jane's fingers stilled. She sighed. It was so quiet here. So different from the noisy, frantic pace of the city. The lazy June afternoon should make her feel tranquil and peaceful. Instead, she felt anxious and panicked.

"You gonna be okay?" Amber asked.

Jane nodded. "You knew about Morgan. That's why you didn't tell me he was coming." She unpinned the silly name tag and pocketed it. "You were matchmaking, weren't you?"

"Sorry." Amber hung her head. "After you'd told me about your lack of—I mean, lackluster—love life, I thought I'd give you a chance to recapture some high school passion. At least see if there was still a spark there."

"When did you find out?"

"Don't be mad, okay?"

"I won't."

"That night after the senior play when you were spending the night with me. You sneaked away around three in the morning."

Jane looked at her. One auburn brow arched in question. "You followed me?"

"Yep. Saw you meet Morgan at the Dairy Palace and get into his car. The way you two were sucking face, I could have taken a flash picture, and you'd never have noticed."

Jane frowned and muttered, "I hate that phrase."

"What? Sucking face?" Amber giggled. She elbowed Jane. "You could have told me, you know."

Jane returned the gesture. "I know. It was just something so—so private. I'd never felt that way before. About any boy." Or since, she could have added for what it was worth.

"I thought at first maybe you were embarrassed about him."

"You certainly don't have a very high opinion of me."

"In light of what just happened in there, which by the way, will have spread all over town by suppertime, I have a hunch Morgan doesn't think you have a very high opinion of *him* either."

Jane scowled. "I don't care what he thinks." The rest of Amber's comment soaked in. She looked at her friend in horror. "You really think there'll be talk about this?"

"Oh, yeah. I'd bet money on it. Maybe not by supper time. It'll at least take until tomorrow for everyone to have heard."

"But . . . but there weren't that many people there."

"Only Miss Mushmak, who doted on Morgan all through school and who was looking daggers at you, Felicia, the principal, a few other teachers, and about a dozen of your former classmates who came in while we were talking with Felicia. You were too busy establishing your female independence to notice them. Oh, and don't forget Morgan's people."

"Morgan's people?" Jane echoed.

"Yes. An attractive Asian woman with glasses—must be his secretary. A young guy in a suit who's got that grad school look about him. And an army tank disguised as a man in a navy suit. Betcha anything he's a bodyguard."

Jane said faintly, "Felicia was right about that too. He really does have an entourage."

"I knew Morgan would arrive by limo since we don't have an airport. I don't see a limo back here, so it must be in the circle drive in front of the school. This is the biggest thing to hit town since the Dixie Super opened."

"My mother's going to kill me," Jane moaned.

"No, she won't. She'll just give you that lecture about how ladies don't make spectacles of themselves."

"I didn't see all those people," Jane protested.

"Yeah. I know. You had eyes only for Morgan."

"I did not!"

"Yeah. You did. Wonder what it's like to suck face with him now?" Amber asked, a sly expression in her eyes.

"I wonder." When Jane realized what she'd said, she hastily rose. "I mean, I don't. I couldn't care less about how he kisses." Ten years ago he could make her dizzy with his kisses. If he was any more skilled now, she'd need medical help.

"I may have made some inappropriate remarks, but I didn't mean anything personal by them. I was just trying to make the point that I am not looking for a husband. I have absolutely no interest in Morgan Sherwood," Jane declared.

"It's good you don't have any feelings for him. That might make it awkward this weekend. Especially since Felicia seems so interested."

Jane's mouth tightened. She couldn't stand the thought of watching Felicia paw him all weekend long. "Actually, I'd kind of planned to spend most of the next few days with my family. I haven't had a chance for much quality time with them lately."

"You were here for Easter, Janie."

"Well, sure, but that was different."

"You're not saying you're scared to be around Morgan for fear you might jump his bones, are you?" Amber needled.

"Certainly not! Just because I had a teenage crush on him doesn't mean I still feel that way. That's in the past. I was just a silly high school girl. I'm a mature woman now."

"Good. Mature women do not run away when they bump into a former lover, do they?"

Jane blushed hotly. "We weren't exactly lovers."

"I know that. But you did like him, though I'm mystified as to why. I mean, you were a cheerleader—one of the school beauties—and he was just a skinny, nerdy kid. Definitely not A-list material."

"I don't know if I can explain it. I never really understood it myself." Jane looked into the distance, remembering, as if it were yesterday, the desire he had awakened in her.

"There was just something about Morgan. It's as if I didn't see his exterior. There was something inside him that . . . that spoke to me—maybe the way people say art speaks to them when they see a painting they just have to possess. I wanted him." She closed her eyes and remembered how badly she'd wanted him.

"And I thought he wanted me," she said softly. "Something in his eyes when he looked at me made me feel hot and cold at the same time. When he said my name, there was a huskiness in his voice that made me feel the same way."

"So desire reared its ugly head." Amber grinned.

"I guess you're right. I was just too innocent then to know what I was feeling."

"Did he ask you out?"

"No. He never did."

"I bet he thought you'd turn him down flat—the nerd and the cheerleader. I can just about guess the jokes you'd have had thrown at you."

"I didn't care. I just wanted to be with him."

"How on earth did it start?" Amber asked.

"Quite innocently. One afternoon I'd stayed late at school. Daddy had to take a prisoner to the court-house over in Franklin Parish and Mom was at some meeting so I didn't have a way home. Morgan offered me a ride."

"I remember, he drove his grandmother's big old Chrysler to school his senior year."

Jane continued, "We started talking. About what was going on in the world—politics, business, art. He was amazing. He knew so much and seemed so much more intelligent or worldly than the other guys. He didn't laugh when I told him I wanted to go to art school in New York." Jane fell silent.

"Go on," Amber encouraged.

"Well, that led to other rides home. Somehow, I found myself creating reasons to stay late on the days he did. I asked him to tutor me in calculus just to continue having a reason to see him. At first, all we did was talk. Then, one evening, I don't know how it happened. He kissed me." She smiled softly. "After that, nothing was the same." She looked over at Amber. "He asked me to meet him late at night. And I did. Crazy, huh?"

"Sounds as if you were crazy in love, Janie."

Emotion clogged Jane's throat. "I guess I was."

"So what happened? If that's how you felt, why aren't you Mrs. Sherwood right now?"

Jane shrugged. "I don't know." She looked at her watch. "I need to get over to Mom's. I promised her I'd be home for dinner with her and Daddy before your party tonight."

"In other words, you don't want to talk about it."

"Let's leave it for now. I need to pull myself together. If I'm lucky, I can get home, visit with the folks, and get away before someone tells Mom about my little *faux pas* today."

"Okay, I'll let you off the hook, but don't even think about skipping town or staying away from the reunion."

Jane sighed. "I promise I'll stick it out. I suppose this happened for the best. I need to put that part of my life in perspective."

"That's what they say on those talk shows," Amber declared. "Face the past, complete the circle, step into the future."

"Sounds reasonable," Jane said.

"Maybe this is keeping you from finding Mr. Right. If that's so, this is the perfect opportunity to let it go. See if there's anything between you and Morgan. Explore all that hot desire you once felt for him—especially since you're old enough to know what it means—and to do something about it."

"Amber, I think it's safe to say that the only thing between Morgan and me now is mutual dislike."

"Well, with Felicia occupying all of Morgan's time, you won't have to be bothered with him. He could be

Mr. Felicia Number Three, remember? Wouldn't that be something?"

"Yeah. That would really be something." Jane felt strangely queasy at the prospect.

JASMINE CRESSWELL

the particular.

want. That wouldn't do, she couldn't, and she
wouldn't manage to do more.

Three

"Janie, I heard that the Tyler boy is home for the
reunion."

Jane suppressed a grin. Her dad's mother had arrived right after supper. She'd been here less than ten
minutes—just long enough to pull her crocheting out
of her oversized white straw handbag and settle onto
the couch next to Jane's mother. The steel crochet
hook flew as Granny J. turned the ball of white cotton
thread into a pineapple doily.

"That's nice, Granny J." Sometimes she wondered
if her mother would be so gung-ho to find her a husband if Granny J.—and the infamous Vernon Ladies
Bridge Club—would stay out of it. Bridge Club! What
a laugh. She wondered if any of the ladies who met
every Wednesday even knew how to play bridge.

Jane tried her best to ignore the two women. She
scanned the section of the weekly newspaper her dad
had passed to her and more or less tuned out her
mother and grandmother. Occasionally, she murmured a yes or a no which was adequate participation
in their free-ranging conversation about the three
thousand inhabitants of Vernon.

Why on earth did anyone bother publishing a

newspaper here? By the time anything hit print, it was old news. With half an ear, Jane caught up on the local gossip—who had died, who was pregnant, who was having an affair. There were no secrets in the small town. If someone sneezed up by Pine Slough, a resident on the south end of town would say, "God bless you."

She found it all amusing—as long as it wasn't about her. Of course, by tomorrow, she thought, her name would be the talk of the good ladies and gentlemen of the town. The story of her little embarrassment this afternoon would be a juicy treat ready to be picked from the convoluted grapevine that wound around the small town.

While she chatted, Jane's mother Brenda pushed her tiny quilting needle through the layers of batting and fabric of the double wedding ring quilt square. It seemed as if her mother had worked on nothing but this since Jane's twenty-fifth birthday. Every time she came for a visit, out came the basket of yellow quilt squares. Each time her mother reminded her that it was for her when she finally wed. Brenda Jones always emphasized the word *finally*.

By this time, Mom must have enough quilt blocks to make a party tent, Jane thought. Still, she enjoyed being in the room with the two older women as they talked and worked. Her quiet father, hiding behind his newspaper, provided a nice contrast to the talkative twosome.

"Bobby Tyler is such a cute boy," Granny J. said. "Don't you think, Brenda?

"Yes, he is, though he's hardly a boy anymore,"

Brenda replied, tying a knot and neatly snipping the thread. She looked over at her daughter. "You could do worse, Janie."

Jane pretended to be engrossed in the newspaper.

"Janie, I think you should invite some of your old friends over. I should have volunteered to host a party as part of the reunion festivities," Brenda said, carefully knotting the thread.

"I don't know, Mom. I think everyone is pretty booked with activities," she hedged. It would not be a good idea to put her mother and her grandmother in the same room with a half dozen unmarried men. Heaven only knew what scheme they might hatch.

"I heard the Tyler boy just broke up with his girl-friend over in Winnsboro," Brenda said.

A disgusted harrumph from Wes Jones and the sound of rustling newspaper saved Jane from answering.

Her grandmother looked up from her crochet, but her fingers never stilled. "Now, Wes, remember what a nice couple he and Janie made back in the eighth grade when he took her to the Valentine Banquet?"

Jane's father lowered his newspaper. "Bobby Tyler's an idiot, Mother. He was then, and he probably still is."

"Just because he misplaced those bags of money when he worked at the bank doesn't mean he's an idiot," Brenda argued.

"Better I think he's an idiot than a thief," Wes muttered, turning back to his newspaper.

Brenda's mouth pursed. "He hasn't been in a speck of trouble since then. He's single, and he's got good prospects. I heard he's district manager for the tractor dealership in Lone Cedar. And he's been to New York City, Janie, so y'all would have something to talk about."

"Sounds as if he could support our Janie comfortably," Granny J. said.

Jane rolled her eyes. "I don't need anyone to support me, Granny. I probably earn more money than Bobby Tyler ever thought about earning. Modern women no longer marry for that reason."

"Then what do they marry for?" Brenda asked, sounding exasperated. "Explain it to me, and maybe I'll understand why you find something wrong with every man you meet."

"You know, Brenda," Granny said. Her voice lowered and she leaned close. "They marry for s-e-x," she spelled out.

Jane covered her mouth to hide her smile. No way could she tell her grandmother that women didn't have to marry for that anymore either. She suppressed a giggle, cleared her throat, and said, "For companionship. What else?"

"And what a wonderful reason," Brenda said. "But you know, dear, when you decide to have children, you may not want to work full time. You might like being at home with your babies. Wouldn't it be a good idea to find someone who made enough money so you wouldn't have to worry about working?" She grinned smugly as if she'd cleverly trapped her daughter.

"If, that is, you decide you want to combine career and family like your sisters," Granny J. interjected.

Jane sighed. As soon as her youngest sister Luci had married four years ago, her mother, assisted by Jane's grandmother, had taken up a new activity to fill her empty nest—finding her oldest daughter a husband. It seemed as if she and Granny J. spent much too much time trying to marry her off. The fact that Jane lived in New York didn't deter them a bit.

"I still don't think Bobby Tyler is a serious contender," Jane muttered. Personally, she agreed with her dad's assessment of Bobby Tyler. He was an idiot—and probably dishonest as well. He'd cheated off her papers in high school. She wouldn't trust him as far as she could throw a bull by the tail, to use her dad's favorite expression.

"What about that nice Morgan Sherwood?" Granny asked.

"No!" Jane unwittingly crumpled the newspaper in her lap as she snapped to attention. "Never!"

"His roots are here even if his grandmother has passed on," Granny J. said, ignoring Jane's protest. "His mother was born and raised here, though no one knows where she is now. Poor Morgan. He had a rotten childhood. It's amazing he turned out so well."

"That's rather a strong reaction, Janie. What's wrong with Morgan?" Brenda asked, her needle still as she stared curiously at her daughter.

Uh-oh. Her mom's interest was piqued. Jane sought to turn the attention from herself. "Whatever happened to Morgan's mom?"

"She was part of that hippie generation who ran away to find herself, but ended up losing herself instead, I reckon," Granny J. answered. "She dropped out and never dropped in again."

"Why isn't Morgan Sherwood a possibility?" Brenda asked, undeterred by her daughter's attempt to change the subject. "He's never been married, and he's easily the richest person in town. Do you know he arrived in a Rolls Royce?"

"No, he didn't, Mom. It was just a limo. Probably a rental."

"Are you sure, Janie? Miss Mamie said it was a Rolls Royce just like in the movies," Granny J. threw in.

"Miss Mamie can hardly see, Granny. She couldn't tell the difference between a Rolls Royce and a Ford Ranger pickup."

"Oh, Miss Mamie didn't actually see it, Janie. Orvelle Thompson's grandson told her about it," Granny J. said.

"The one who got arrested for driving under the influence on graduation night?" Brenda asked, finally shifting her probing eyes from her daughter.

"No, the one who got his ear pierced on the band trip, and his daddy made him take the earring out."

Jane's tension eased as she listened to their discussion about Orvelle's grandson. That was something she adored about southerners. When they mentioned a person, they always gave you a bit of information that placed the person according to family, age, and background. She grinned as the two women continued.

"Oh, you mean Charles Junior," Brenda said.

"As I was saying, Orvelle's grandson Charles Junior—he's the same one who got caught toilet-papering old man Winfrey's yard, by the way—he heard about the Rolls Royce from his mother who was driving by the school this afternoon.''

"It's not a Rolls Royce," Jane said between clenched teeth.

"All I know is what Miss Mamie told me," Granny argued. "She said Charles Junior told her about Morgan's Rolls Royce when he put the groceries in the trunk of her car. He told her that only Morgan's Rolls Royce had a bigger trunk than her Caddy."

"Miss Mamie's car?" Jane frowned. "Good heavens! Surely she isn't still driving? She was nearly blind when I was a kid."

"Now, Janie, don't be so critical," Granny said. "Poor Mamie can't give up her car. This isn't New York City, dear. We don't have all those taxis in Vernon. If Miss Mamie didn't drive, she wouldn't be able to get to the Ladies Club every week."

"Don't worry, dear," Brenda Jones said, calmly. "She never goes over five miles an hour."

"That's right," Granny interjected. "And folks in town know to get out of the way when they see the tail fins of that big blue Caddy."

"Daddy, why don't you do something about Miss Mamie? She shouldn't be driving with her eyesight that bad."

Wes lowered his newspaper. "I had her driver's license revoked," Wes said. "But short of throwing a ninety-year-old woman in jail, what can I do? She promised not to go beyond a ten-block radius of her home. So I posted some signs around for people to watch out for her."

"Sometimes I think everyone in this town is nuts," Jane muttered, convinced that more than mere geography separated her hometown from the rest of the world.

When the phone rang, Brenda rose to answer it.

"Janie, before you discount Morgan Sherwood for some trivial reason," Granny J. said, "I want you to remember something. He's rich. My momma always told me that it's just as easy to fall in love with a rich man as a poor one."

Wes harrumphed and rustled the newspaper.

Jane let loose a long-suffering sigh.

"What did Jane Louise do this afternoon?" Brenda asked sharply into the phone.

Jane glanced guiltily at her mother. The cat was being let out of the bag even as she watched.

Living up to her mother's idea of ladylike behavior was difficult. Back in high school, Jane had decided there was nothing worse than a born-again lady like her mother. She found it hard to believe that Brenda Jones was the same person as the California girl in the hippie sandals and love beads in the photo her dad carried in his wallet.

"I think I'll take off for Amber's now." Jane planted a hasty kiss on her grandmother's cheek and on her dad's forehead, the only part visible over the top of the newspaper.

"Dinner was delicious, Mom." She ignored her mother's frantic waves to stay where she was and rushed to the front door. "I should be home early."

"If you get a chance, bring some of those unattached young people back with you," Granny J. said.

"Just don't bring Bobby Tyler," Wes Jones grumbled.

Her dad's remark surprised a laugh from her. Brenda's hobby of finding her daughter a husband was neatly counterbalanced by Wes's ability to find something negative about each of Brenda's candidates.

"That Sherwood boy's okay though," Wes added. "You can bring him if you want to."

The moon shone brightly, illuminating the porch railing where Jane and Amber sat.

"What's the matter, Janie?"

"I just needed some fresh air." She didn't want to admit she was still musing about her dad's parting comment.

"You don't seem like your usual self," Amber said lightly.

"Guess I'm not in a party mood."

"It's Morgan, isn't it? What *did* happen between you two back in high school? Come on. It'll help to talk about it."

Jane sighed. "Maybe you're right. I told you I was in love—really in love with him. I'd have given myself to him—heart, soul, and body—if he'd asked. I was building air castles, signing my name Mrs. Morgan Sherwood, Jane Sherwood, Jane Jones-Sherwood, all the usual silly stuff. Then one day, he just cut me out of his life. Poof. I was history. And I never knew why. I've never been able to figure out how anyone could turn his emotions off so quickly—and so completely."

"Y'all didn't have a fight or anything?"

"Nothing." Jane shook her head. "He wouldn't talk to me at school. Just looked through me as if I didn't exist. He wouldn't take my phone calls at home. It was as if I didn't exist for him anymore. Then a week later, we graduated from high school, and he left town. I've never heard from him again."

"That's crazy."

"I was devastated." Jane swallowed the knot of emotion. Suddenly, at home again, with Morgan in the next room, the pain was as fresh as if it had happened yesterday.

Amber squeezed her shoulder. "I can remember thinking something was wrong. But I couldn't ask you about it because it was a secret. I was afraid you'd be mad if you'd known I had followed you."

Jane shrugged eloquently. "Well, eventually, I got over Morgan. Life goes on—even when you're a heartbroken teenager. And that's all there is to it."

"That's not all there is. There's still something there. I could see it when you looked at Morgan this afternoon. And if it was over, you wouldn't be doing your best to avoid him tonight. You've ducked out here every time he comes within ten feet."

"You're imagining things," Jane scoffed. She should have gotten over her high school heartbreak years ago, and by golly, she would. She planned to devote every waking hour to the task.

"You will never get over him until you finish it."

"Finish what? There's nothing to finish," Jane protested. "I'm tired of discussing this. Let's go back in."

"If there wasn't unfinished business that kept you

from falling in love, you'd have found someone by now, and your mom and granny wouldn't be match-making."

"Okay. Okay. Maybe you're right." Jane sighed. "This afternoon Granny J. and Mom mentioned Morgan. They started that business about it being as easy to fall in love with a rich man as a poor one."

"Well, that is good advice," Amber said. "I'm going to tell my daughter the same thing—when I have one."

That brought a smile to Jane's face. "Yeah, but somehow I don't think you can command your heart that way. If it were that easy to make yourself fall in love, I'd have done so long ago. And I'd have completely forgotten Morgan."

"So you admit you still care," Amber crowed. "Janie, you need to reopen that pending file and let nature take its course."

"Would you quit babbling like a talk show host?"

"Listen to me. Back in high school, the logical course would have been for you to continue seeing Morgan. Eventually, you two would have succumbed to your lust. Right?"

"Probably. I was certain, deep in my soul, that he was meant for me."

"So play it out. Get the lust out in the open and be done with it. There's probably part of you still wondering what it would have been like. That mystique has a hold on you. So sleep with him if that's what it takes to get him out of your system."

Jane was shocked. "You're joking, right?"

Amber slowly shook her head. "Hey, the more I think about it . . ."

"You know, it might be the best way to get over him." Excited, Amber grabbed Jane's arm. "I think that's what you should do. Seduce him this weekend, and you won't have to wonder anymore. Then dump him Monday morning. It's also the perfect revenge." Her grin surprised a wry laugh from Jane.

Teasingly, she said, "Okay, Amber, I'll do it. I'll seduce Morgan Sherwood within an inch of his life."

A floorboard creaked. Amber sat up straighter. "Is anyone there?"

No one answered.

"Maybe we should lower our voices," she suggested.

"Yeah, I wouldn't want the whole town to know I'm plotting against their favorite son," Jane said with a weak smile. What little humor she'd seen in the conversation vanished.

"Plotting to seduce their favorite son isn't quite the same as plotting against him," Amber argued. "He'll get something out of this too. So how do you plan to get him in the sack?"

Jane was silent. This whole conversation was stupid. But joking about it took some of the pain away.

"Amber, you are incorrigible. Why don't you go inside while I sit out here and figure out how to get him between the sheets?"

"Okay. I need to see to my guests anyway. After you figure out how to get him in bed, you'd better plan how you'll tell him to kiss off come Monday. After all, you don't want to be stuck with him. He's probably lousy in bed."

"Oh," Jane said breezily, "I'll just toss him away like a worn-out shoe."

Amber grinned in return. "If any woman can do it, you can."

"I know. I'm such a man-eater," Jane said in a dry voice.

"He's no match for a woman of your experience," Amber said.

Jane laughed, but it sounded brittle to her ears. "You know, you're probably right. I bet he is a lousy lover. After all, he's a multimillionaire. He spends all his time making money—not love."

"He's no challenge at all," Amber said. "How hard can it be to wrap a rich workaholic around your little finger? After this weekend, you can add him to your conquests."

"Go on, Amber. I'll be back in shortly."

Jane kept her smile in place until Amber was gone. Then she sighed. Too bad her friend's scheme appealed to her so much. Just the thought of falling into bed with him made her heart race. In high school, even when he'd been tall and skinny, he'd made her want him. Now . . . wow! His appeal was even stronger, unfortunately. Maybe yielding to temptation and indulging in what had been forbidden in high school *was* the cure for a bad case of loving Morgan Sherwood.

It certainly was true that eavesdroppers never heard good of themselves, Morgan thought. So Jane planned to bed him and then boot him out?

When he'd heard Jane declare her plan to seduce him, wild horses couldn't have made him retrace his steps and enter the house. The creaky floorboard had nearly given him away, but the side porch was deeply shadowed and the huge urns of Boston fern provided good cover. The two women were too busy plotting to be curious enough to investigate the sound. He'd heard every damning word they had said.

Fifteen minutes later, his anger had cooled enough for him to settle into the porch swing and focus the power of his brain. So Jane expected him to be lousy in bed, huh? She thought she could wrap him around her little finger. Everything—every insult—rang in his ears. He'd enjoy showing her exactly how wrong she was.

She'd used him in high school, and now she thought to complete the seduction she'd begun ten years ago, apparently just to prove she could, since no calculus grade hung in the balance.

Sleep with him and then drop him on Monday? Ha! It was time someone gave the scheming beauty her comeuppance. And he was just the man to do it.

Morgan pulled his cell phone from his coat pocket and flipped the wafer-thin electronic marvel open. In less than a minute he was connected to the private number of one of the most beautiful starlets in Hollywood.

"Serena? How would you like a fun-filled weekend in a small town chock full of real people? No Hollywood phonies, just me and the gang and three thousand adoring fans?" Morgan laughed at her reply. Then he explained what he wanted. "Do this for me, and I'll double my contribution to the scholarship fund you've started."

When she agreed, he gave her instructions. "Yeah, it'll be fun. I can't wait to see you too." More importantly, he couldn't wait for Jane to get an eyeful of the beauty who'd recently shared the silver screen with the movie's most famous secret agent.

So Jane wanted to play hardball with people's emotions, huh? Just like she'd done in high school. Well, he wasn't a gawky teenager anymore. He could teach her a thing or two about lovemaking—regardless of her legion of admirers, he fumed.

Then, come Monday, Morgan thought, *we'll see who tells who to kiss off.*

Four

Nearly four dozen people had crammed into Amber and Steve Chalmers's home by the time Morgan returned to the party. The noise level equaled that from the trading floor at the commodities exchange, he thought, wincing as someone cranked up the volume on the sound system.

He concentrated on external things, a technique he'd developed to control his emotions. Calmly he analyzed the Chalmers's bungalow. He rather liked it, he decided. It was warm and homey—something his own penthouse seemed to lack despite paying decorators an absolute fortune.

Here, the huge living room with its overstuffed couches and chairs in a muted gold velvet invited one to sit beneath the slow-turning ceiling fan and chat. At the moment, every seat was taken—nearly two deep with many of the women sitting in the laps of their husbands or boyfriends.

Morgan leaned against the pillar supporting the arched double doorway that opened into the dining room. Where was the devious duo? he wondered, looking around. He found Amber and her husband Steve chatting with Berkley and Verna Wright. Jane was nowhere in sight.

He couldn't be more pleased that Verna seemed to be as attracted to Berk as his friend was to her. It was about time Berk got interested in a woman. Good thing Verna wasn't anything like the green-eyed witch who was plotting against him.

Morgan walked over to the dining table and served himself a cup of the pink punch. Taking a sip, he grimaced at the syrupy sweet concoction. At the moment, he needed something much stronger. Judging by Penny's expression, he thought looking toward where she sat in the den, she agreed with him.

Penny Tranh seemed so miserable Morgan regretted having forced her to come here. She stared morosely at her own cup of punch, looking uncomfortably isolated as she sat alone in a rocking chair by the brick hearth. He frowned, suddenly forgetting his own situation in his concern for her.

He walked across the pegged wood floor and crouched by the oak rocker. "What's the matter, Penny? Don't care for pink reunion punch?"

"Punch? What a misnomer," she sniffed. "There's more punch in a glass of three-day-old soda than in this stuff."

"Bear up, old girl," Morgan teased. "Maybe we can find a fruit jar full of moonshine for you to sample."

"Ha. Like I'm dumb enough to drink something these southern boys of yours make in some backwoods distillery."

"Actually, I don't know if any of these guys have ever seen a jar of moonshine," Morgan said. "The only thing you're likely to get in this dry parish is some of that ninety octane coffee back at the inn later."

"I'd lay odds that a strong cup of coffee will be the highlight of this evening," she muttered, looking around with a pained expression. "Who on earth plays country music at a party?" she added in a whisper.

Morgan shrugged. "People who like country music, I suppose."

Penny shot him a withering glare. "You're not paying me enough to subject me to this kind of torture, Morgan."

He grinned, amused at what she saw as an insult to her sophisticated, urban sensibilities.

"You all right, Morgan?" she suddenly asked, frowning.

"Sure. I'm fine. Just enjoying the punch," he said, taking another sip of the awfully sweet stuff.

"You look—funny," she said, shrugging her shoulders.

"It's just your imagination, Penny. Where's Carlos?" he asked, changing the subject.

"He's off chatting with Jim Bob or Jim Tom or Jim somebody about cotton futures. As if that kid knows more about agricultural commodities than I do," she huffed, making it apparent that she was insulted.

"Ah, I think I begin to see why your nose is so out of joint. It's a man's world in this little corner of the state, isn't it?"

Penny snorted. "You're telling me? This is as bad as a visit to my relatives. I hate to tell you this, Morgan, but your old hometown is stuck back in the fifties. I'm surprised the women here don't wear hats and white gloves to the supermarket."

"No, I think they repealed that law," Morgan joked.

"Why on earth you wanted to come to this is beyond me."

"I had my reasons. Come on. Loosen up. You might have some fun." He planned to, he thought, slowly nodding.

"Don't tell me you're enjoying this excruciating trip down memory lane?"

Morgan considered. "Not yet, but ask me again tomorrow. I should have a different answer by then."

"And would that woman at the reception this afternoon have any connection to your planned pleasure?"

He didn't even pretend he didn't know who she was referring to. He nodded. "Could be."

"Who is she?"

"Just a friend from high school."

"Some friend!"

Morgan laughed—short and cynical. "Enough about her. I want you to cheer up, Penny." He pointed across the room. "You see that guy in the light blue golf shirt?" At her nod, he said, "That's Don Gage. He graduated third in our class. His dad was the founder and president of the local bank. Now Don's the president—and he's single. I'll just mosey over there and let it drop that you sold the highs last month in the crude oil market and made a cool ten grand trading your own account. He'll beat a path to your side."

"Yeah, probably to ask me to open an account with his dinky little bank," Penny grumbled. Then she sighed. "Okay, he's better than nothing. But you tell

Berk and Carlos I'm leaving at eleven o'clock to-night—with them or without them."

"Berk might have something to say about that," Morgan said, grinning.

"Won't do him a bit of good. I've got the car keys," Penny said, reaching into her jacket pocket and pull-ing out the rental agency key tag. She waved it and nodded as if to say, "So there."

Morgan laughed. "I'm not getting between you and those two gentlemen—especially Berkley. You're on your own, kiddo."

"Go mosey, Morgan," Penny said, pocketing the car keys.

Morgan chatted with his former classmate who ran the bank. To Gage's credit, he didn't give Morgan a hard sell about putting some of his money in the local bank. In fact, Gage, a quiet guy even in high school, he remembered, was very pleasant and more than will-ing to talk to Penny.

Morgan suspected Penny's elegant looks figured more in Gage's thoughts than any mention of Penny's killing in the commodities market. Penny needed to be less of a workaholic, he thought. It would do her good to have some fun. He watched Don Gage walk toward her. Maybe Don would provide that for her this weekend.

His next stop was Berkley. He managed to chat a bit about mundane matters with Amber and Steve. The temptation to tell Amber what he thought of her and her friend Jane was strong, but he suppressed it. He'd get his revenge when he saw the look on Jane's face Monday morning.

Morgan complimented the couple on the great party, then passed on Penny's message to Berk. To his surprise, Berk didn't even frown. *He must be having too good a time to get upset,* Morgan thought, pleased. This weekend was working out pretty well for Berkley at least. He left them after a bit and went in search of Carlos.

When he found the younger man and told him what Penny had said, he looked a little worried, but Morgan laughed and reassured him that Penny's bark was a lot worse than her bite. Carlos, as the new guy on the staff, wasn't quite sure what to make of the joking and horseplay that went on among the key personnel of Sherwood Investments. He was young and conscientious, taking his position seriously, sometimes too seriously, but Morgan was certain he'd lighten up as time went by and adapt to the sometimes quirky behavior of the people in the company.

Morgan passed the next hour chatting with practically every person at the party. He'd glimpsed a flash of red between the guests, but Jane seemed to be a step ahead of him as he moved through the room. He frowned. Didn't she know she was losing valuable seduction time? Or maybe the task was so distasteful, she couldn't bring herself to do it. His eyes narrowed, but he kept a tight rein on his anger.

Duties done, it was time, he decided, to dump the now-warm fruit punch. Then he planned to treat himself to another breath of fresh air and some quiet before he put the moves on Jane.

At least everyone seemed to have forgotten that he could buy and sell the whole town. They'd begun to relax and joke with him, seeming to accept him finally as someone no more important than any other former classmate. Several had commented on the scene with Jane, ribbing him good-naturedly.

He poured the drink down the kitchen drain, set his glass in the sink and turned. That's when he saw Jane. She was silhouetted in the doorway leading to the porch. His gut tightened. Somehow it wasn't right that she looked so damn good—better than she had in high school. She'd been pretty then, but now there was something about her that made her even more desirable. There was a certain sensuality in her green eyes that intrigued him. And probably every other man out there.

He couldn't help but notice that her body was fuller than in high school, but full in the best way—naturally curved and graceful. She carried herself with the same beautiful posture that had captivated him ten years ago. Even then she had seemed so poised and self-assured, as if she knew exactly what she was doing and where she was going.

Morgan watched her intently. She'd removed her red jacket. The blue tank top, or whatever women called those little bits of nothing that passed for a shirt, hugged her curves gently, revealing more of her pale ivory skin than he was comfortable with.

He heard a woman's high heels tapping over the kitchen tile and smelled Felicia's rather heavy perfume. She seemed to have radar where he was concerned.

"Morgan, so you're hiding in the kitchen!" she crowed.

He forced a grin. "You caught me, Felicia."

"Don't I wish." She winked at him as she brushed past him, breasts skimming the arm of his navy double-breasted jacket.

Morgan refrained from sighing and stepped away, not wanting another glimpse of the twin marvels of her breasts bulging above the black strapless cocktail dress she nearly wore. She'd already treated him to an eyeful the moment he, Penny, Carlos, and Berk had arrived at the party. Poor Carlos had flushed guiltily and jerked his eyes from her neckline when he'd realized that Morgan was watching him with amusement.

Felicia dumped her glass of punch also. "Too much sugar," she said. "Bad for the body."

Felicia started talking about her favorite subject—herself—so Morgan easily tuned her out and pursued his own thoughts which centered around Jane.

Covertly, he kept an eye on her as someone called to her. She turned from the doorway and walked over to a man. Morgan cursed silently. When had Jason Lombardo slithered in?

Morgan kept a tight rein on his emotions and carefully schooled his expression to show no anger. How fitting that Jason, the school's star quarterback, and Jane, the head cheerleader, were once again talking and laughing together. Maybe he should thank Jason for the lesson he'd taught Morgan.

Jane's laughter caught his attention. He could have been on a crowded street, and he'd still have recognized her laugh. In an instant, he was back in the old Chrysler as he and Jane had parked behind the now-defunct ice cream stand. He remembered how her laughter bubbled through the darkness that enveloped them. She'd always laughed at his jokes.

He felt the tiny hairs on the back of his neck raise as he recalled how his blood had pounded when he'd kissed her the first time—drinking the sound of her laughter into his mouth, his lungs, and his body, absorbing it the way he wanted to absorb her until they were one.

Why hadn't she ever married? Probably having too much fun with all her lovers, he thought darkly. He'd nearly been her lover. That thought sent a shaft of pain through him. Once he'd thought he'd be her first—and her last.

"Morgan? I don't think you heard a word I said," Felicia complained.

"Of course I did," Morgan lied. Would Jane laugh like that when she dropped him like an old shoe?

"I need to visit the little girl's room," Felicia said with a wink. "If you like, we could probably both squeeze in there. I'm sure there's a lock on the door."

"Sounds like an interesting proposition," Morgan said, falling back on business babble. "I'll have my people get back to you on that after due consideration."

"What?" Felicia snapped.

Morgan's attention returned to Felicia. What had the flirty fitness queen been talking about?

"Well, send me a memo when you decide," Felicia snapped. She spun on her heel and stalked off.

Morgan watched her go with a feeling of relief. Though he was used to being the object of female attention, he didn't particularly enjoy it when the woman dishing out the attention had dollar signs in her eyes.

He turned to look at Jane again, but she wasn't there any longer. Morgan looked around the room. She wasn't inside at all. Neither was Lombardo, he realized with a flash of anger. He looked toward the doorway. Someone had turned off the porch light. Were they out there in the dark? Together? He imagined her in Lombardo's arms and nearly went ballistic at the thought.

Mouth tight with suppressed anger, Morgan rushed outside. Though the front porch was dark, he could easily see it was empty. Softly, he walked around to the side where he'd hidden earlier.

Knowing how deep the shadows were, he investigated but couldn't see anyone. He followed the wrap-around porch to the back. He saw Jane before she saw him. She was sitting in the swing. Alone. Relief slowed his footsteps.

Morgan knew he should go back inside and wait for her to make the first move. But he told himself that she would never get him seduced at the rate she was going.

Maybe he should give her a little help.

Five

Footsteps brought Jane from her reverie. The edge of the porch was bathed in moonlight, but shadows obscured the man who walked toward her. She recognized Morgan anyway. He didn't speak a word as he approached. Her eyes sought his, but the darkness shielded him. Her heart fluttered and then settled into a deeper, stronger rhythm. She was nearly breathless with anticipation of the impending confrontation.

Conflicting emotions battled for prominence. Did she want to demand an explanation for his behavior ten years ago? Or did she want to seduce him, as Amber had jokingly suggested, and rid herself of the past once and for all? Judging by the way her heart beat faster, seduction was definitely the more appealing of the two options.

"So this is where you're hiding," Morgan said.

Jane frowned. Another option she hadn't considered presented itself. She could give him the dressing-down that he seemed to be begging for. The words trembled on the end of her tongue.

"I am not hiding." Jane sat up straighter. "I have no reason to hide."

"Are you sure about that? Seems as if you have the unfortunate habit of insulting people."

"And you have the unfortunate habit of smirking," she said with saccharine sweetness. "Of the two, I'd say being bluntly honest is by far the lesser of two evils."

"Maybe smirking is in the eye of the beholder?" he asked, leaning against the side of the house and folding his arms.

"Don't you have someone inside to impress?" Jane snapped.

"What's the matter? Am I interrupting your self-imposed isolation?"

"Do you work at saying the most annoying thing possible or does it come naturally?" Jane didn't give him a chance to reply. "I'm not punishing myself by staying out here. I'm merely getting a breath of fresh air."

Morgan inhaled deeply. "Yeah. I see what you mean. I'd forgotten how honeysuckle smelled in the darkness."

"I don't imagine there's very much honeysuckle in Los Angeles."

"I'd guess even less than in New York." He grinned. "Even if there were, I doubt I could smell it on the sixtieth floor."

"My, my. The penthouse suite no doubt." She knew she was being snide, but she couldn't seem to help herself. "Why don't you just go around with a photocopy of your bank balance? That would be a much more direct way to impress people."

Morgan didn't seem to take offense. Instead, he

laughed. "I don't remember your being quite so out-spoken in high school."

"People change," Jane stated flatly.

"But seldom," he said.

"Just because you tried your best to embarrass me this afternoon doesn't mean I'm intimidated by you or your money."

"Calm down. I was the one who was the victim. You were the one slinging mud."

"I was not slinging mud. I was just trying to make a point to Felicia."

"Yeah, that I don't impress you and that you can get milk without buying a cow."

"I didn't know you were even in town—much less sneaking up behind me! Believe it or not, I'd never have said that if I thought anyone other than Felicia was listening."

"Is that supposed to be an apology?"

"It's as much an apology as you're going to get." And more than he'd ever given her, she thought, grinding her teeth.

"I always thought that line about the cow referred to a man getting something from a woman without marrying her."

He stepped over to the swing. Before she knew what he was doing, he sat next to her. Shocked, Jane started to rise.

"Not afraid to sit next to me, are you?"

He couldn't have said anything better to guarantee that she would remain right where she was. Lips tightening in annoyance, Jane fell back onto the seat, jarring the swing.

"Of course not," she said. But survival instinct made her move as far from him as possible until she crowded the other arm of the wooden swing with about a foot of space between them.

Morgan pushed with his feet, setting the swing in motion. The chains squeaked gently, a homey, cozy sound in the darkness.

Jane knew she was in trouble now, but she couldn't seem to extricate herself.

"I was thinking about that cow aphorism. If you're going to use that in your next speech, you should really change the gender. Maybe say that you can get service from the bull without marrying him."

"You're being deliberately crude and insulting," Jane said, in as cold a tone as she could manage over the hammering of her heart.

"Insulting? What was that you said? I don't impress you—not ten years ago and not now? That's insulting."

Jane bit her lip. Surely that wasn't pain she heard in his voice? "I didn't mean that quite the way it came out."

He clutched his heart. "Oh, my! Say it isn't so! You're not apologizing, are you?"

Her ire rose anew at his melodramatic posturing. "Quit acting like a jerk."

His quiet chuckle broke the tension between them. They swung in silence for several minutes.

Maybe she should let it go. She had a sneaking suspicion that she, too, wasn't behaving very well. No one who knew her would believe she could be anything other than pleasant, calm, and logical. Good thing none of her friends could see the way she was behaving in her hometown. For some reason, Morgan seemed to bring out the worst in her.

Jane took a calming breath and resolved to make peace with him. It was silly to be influenced by what had happened when they were kids, she told herself.

"Morgan, what are you doing back here?" she asked calmly.

"I needed a breath of fresh air. You're right about there being too many people inside now."

"I don't mean here on the porch. I mean back in Vernon. Why did you come to the reunion?"

Morgan didn't look at her. He couldn't tell her why he'd really come back this weekend. Not now. Not when he knew what she planned to do. Instead, he said, "Let's just say I wanted to show everyone in town that I made good."

"I think they already knew that."

In a strained voice, he couldn't help but ask, "Did you know, Jane?"

"I'd heard, but I didn't know if it was true. You know how everyone in this town talks. Each time a story goes around, it gets more exaggerated."

"Yeah. The guy who created the joke about spreading news by telegraph, telephone, or tell-a-woman must have been from here."

"You've really amazed everyone in this town with your success."

"What about you? Did I surprise you too?" Did she remember the dreams he'd shared with her?

"No. I can't say you did. Even in high school I recognized something about you that hinted of"—she paused, then laughed lightly, as if making a joke—"shall we say greatness?"

He smiled as well. "I don't know if I would call it greatness, but I'd definitely call it driven. I had something to prove."

Hastily, Morgan added, "To the town." He thought about how he'd waited ten years to come back—ten years of hard work amassing his fortune—just to show her. Just so he could lay the world at her feet. During all those years of hard work, he'd never allowed himself to think that she would marry someone else. In his fantasy, she'd always been available and had always welcomed him with open arms. Unlike real life.

"Well, you certainly did. The stretch limo was a nice touch."

He saw that she was smiling. He grinned. "I thought it might be the icing on the cake."

He was enjoying their conversation too much, he thought, needing to remind himself of why he had come out here. So far, Jane hadn't made one single move that could be construed as seductive. What was she waiting for? Maybe it was time for that nudge.

"Jane, there's something I think we should talk about."

Startled, Jane looked at him quickly. She'd been thinking about Amber's suggestion—seducing Morgan.

"Yes? What is it?" She tried to focus her attention on the present and quit fantasizing about that enormously appealing prospect. Maybe he was finally going to apologize. Something in Jane softened at the prospect. She smiled gently. She'd waited years to hear him explain his behavior and beg her forgiveness. Here it came.

"Yes, Morgan, go on."

"Do you get the feeling that we have some unfinished business left from high school?"

Hot color filled her face. She was glad of the obscuring darkness. How odd that he used the same phrase Amber had used.

"I, uh, don't quite know what you mean."

"Back then, I didn't have much to offer a girl like you."

Jane frowned. "A girl like me? What do you mean by that?"

"You know. You were a cheerleader with lots of boyfriends. I was an outsider in this town, sent here to live after my parents took off for God knows where." He shrugged. "Between my grandmother's Social Security and my job at the gas station, we could barely keep food on the table. So I never had the money to treat you the way your other boyfriends did."

Jane was floored. Was that why he'd rejected her before the prom? Because he couldn't afford the tux, the flowers, the limo that the other kids considered standard? How shallow! And how shallow he must have thought she was.

"So I thought maybe we could relive those days— and nights." His voice dropped low until it was a sexy purr. "I have more than enough money to show you a good time now."

"I don't think I understand what you're getting at," she said carefully, trying not to break the fragile truce that seemed to have developed between them. "But I do know I don't care for your insinuation."

"I'm not insinuating anything. I'm stating very plainly and baldly—you're favorite kind of honesty, remember?—that you can have me and my money."

Jane's mouth dropped open. Then it snapped closed to keep the torrent of words from slipping out.

"For the weekend."

Her astonishment knew no bounds. The same could be said for his crassness. Jane was speechless.

He slid over a couple of inches. "Remember how we used to talk for hours? Didn't you like those long conversations?"

"Yes, they were nice, but—" she sputtered, still at a loss as to how to reply to his unflattering proposition.

"Nice?" He slid another inch closer. "They were better than nice. We have the whole weekend ahead of us. It's been ages since I had such meaningful conversations."

To Jane's consternation, she could feel her pulse speeding up as she listened to him. His voice had now dropped to a whisper.

"Yes. I really enjoyed talking about national events, and business, and . . . and stuff," she finished lamely. Though she tried to remember how angry she was, his nearness, his low, sexy voice, the intensity in his eyes were too much for her.

"They were great." Morgan slid another inch closer. The swing rocked back. "Then there were those other times. In the dark. In my car. Behind the ice cream stand."

A shudder rushed through Jane. She prayed he didn't notice how he was affecting her respiration.

"Sitting in my grandmother's old Chrysler," he whispered.

The words seemed to float through the air, landing on Jane's nerve endings. She felt his hip touch hers and realized he'd closed the distance between them. The heat resulting from his nearness transformed her anger, creating smoldering desire from its embers.

"I think I hear someone calling me," Jane whispered in a last-ditch effort to save herself.

"I don't think so."

What if he touched her?

What if he didn't?

She hadn't really thought to seduce him. But here he was, looking and sounding so incredibly seductive himself in the dark.

"Don't you ever wonder what it would have felt like?" he whispered.

"What what would have felt like?" She silently cursed the fact that her voice shook. She saw his teeth gleam in the darkness.

"You know. *It.*"

"No. No. I never did," she lied, hoping he didn't remember how frantic she'd been to know exactly how *it* would feel with him. Praying that he never found out how much she thought about it still.

"I really need to go. I promised Amber I'd start cleaning up." Yet she made no effort to rise. It took more energy than she possessed to overcome the strange lethargy that seemed to have hold of her. Being with him, hearing his soft, alluring voice in the dark sapped her will. The only thing that existed in this moment was the siren call of desire.

Blood flowed into and pooled in all the erogenous zones that longed for his touch. Oh, yes! She remembered how it had felt to be beneath him—flattened on the front seat of his old car, with him deliciously heavy on top of her. She'd wanted so much more, but she'd been shy and hadn't known how to push him beyond his control. If he'd asked, she'd have given him anything—everything. That's how foolishly in love she'd been. He'd been the one with the good sense to stop before they passed the point of no return.

"You're not exactly behaving the way I thought you would," he said. "What's the matter? Lose your nerve?"

His question made no sense, but Jane was too enthralled to question him. If she didn't get away from him, she was going to make a fool of herself.

"It's a little chilly out here now. I was out before and that's why I went inside," she babbled. With a near-hysterical giggle, she added, "In and out, all night long."

When the double entendre dawned on her, she clapped her hands over her imprudent mouth. But it was too late.

"In and out?" he breathed. "All night long?"

"I meant inside and outside the house," she hastily explained. That just made it worse. She fell silent, refusing to say another word. Talk about a Freudian slip. Her mouth had done nothing but get her in trouble since she'd arrived in Vernon.

He turned and placed his hands on her upper arms.

"All that must make you pretty tired. Going in and out of the house, I mean."

"What are you doing?" His touch seared her.

"I thought I'd warm you up." He ran his hands up and down her arms as if to warm her. "You're really shivering."

If he didn't quit touching her, she was going to lose her mind. Or her control. Or both.

The voice of rationalization was as seductive as his touch. It whispered to her that she'd never get him out of her system until she went to bed with him.

"Here." Morgan removed his jacket and before she could protest, he draped it over her shoulders. That just made matters worse. She felt enveloped in his scent—his warmth. She inhaled deeply and felt dizzy. She looked up. Her gaze was snared by his.

"Actually, I think it's a bit warm tonight," Morgan said. He loosened his tie. His eyes never left hers. He pulled the length of silk free.

Jane couldn't have looked away if her life had depended on it.

One-handed, he unfastened the collar button, then two more shirt buttons. She swallowed, and her eyes dropped to the opening in his shirt. In the dim light, she caught a glimpse of dark chest hair and her libido went berserk. Beads of sweat popped out on her forehead.

"Here!" She thrust the coat at him. "I'm not a bit cold anymore." Even to her own ears, her voice sounded strained and breathless.

Morgan grinned at her—that sexy, meet-you-in-the-bedroom kind of look. Jane suddenly realized that was the same way he'd looked at her in high school. At eighteen, she just hadn't known exactly what that meant. She'd only known it made the pulse pound low in her body.

He stuffed the tie in his coat pocket and tossed the jacket over the wooden arm of the swing next to him.

"I promised Amber I'd help, uh . . ." Jane said, her voice strained.

"Clean up. Yeah, I know. You mentioned it. I'm sure she'll understand and get someone else to do it."

She could feel the warmth of his hip right up next to hers. His arm brushed against hers, making her nerve endings tingle. She was glad it was dark enough that he couldn't see her tightly beaded nipples beneath the blue silk. They were a dead giveaway as to her state of arousal. Her breath came in short gasps as she tried to marshal her defenses.

What was he doing to her? That sneaky voice of rationalization whispered, *He's giving you what you really want so be quiet and enjoy it.*

"I've never stopped thinking about you," Morgan said, his voice even lower and sexier.

"You haven't?"

"No. I remember every kiss. Every caress. Every touch. You've haunted my dreams," he said with raw honest emotion.

"And you mine," she replied softly, surprised enough to be honest with him.

"I had nothing to offer you in high school," he said.

"I wanted nothing except you."

Morgan felt a stab of anger at her reply. So she'd finally decided to play along, huh? Somehow it wasn't quite right that he had to set himself up for her to seduce him.

"What we had was so special," he said. At least it had been to him. "We never got a chance to let those feelings grow and mature."

When she didn't say anything, he added, "But let's not talk about the past when the present is here. We're mature adults. We don't have to restrain our appetites. That fruit is not forbidden any longer." His hand moved. The tip of his index finger glided up her arm.

She gratified him with a shiver. He wondered if it was real or just playacting. Maybe it was real. He'd learned a lot about women over the years. Some things a woman just couldn't fake.

"And," he whispered, "I find myself ravenous to taste what was once forbidden."

His fingertip skimmed down her arm, then up again. He heard her breath—heavy and rapid. He smiled. So she was such a hot number that she took pleasure in seducing a man for a joke.

His fingertip traced a slow circle on her shoulder. Over and over, he drew circles. Her breath came quicker. She wanted him, he knew. But did she want him as much as his hard body wanted her?

Thickly, he said, "In high school, we never got beyond a few kisses." He could tell her the exact number if she wanted to know.

Jane leaned toward him.

"A few caresses." His finger swooped up the side of her neck, and along her jawbone.

She moaned. The sound was low and ragged, startling Morgan. The tip of her tongue came out to wet her lips. And nearly made him forget why he was doing this.

"But we always stopped before going—"

Morgan gulped. He wanted her. He'd planned to just tease her and then dump her, but why waste a good seduction? He'd die if he couldn't have her in his bed.

"Before going all the way."

His fingertip traced her slightly parted, moist lips, then slowly, ever so slowly, slid down the column of her neck only to halt at the scoop neck of her royal blue shell.

Her breasts rose and fell with excitement. He hesitated suddenly, questioning what he was doing. Questioning his intentions. Just because she was a seductive tease didn't mean he had to play the same game.

"Are you going to talk all night or kiss me?" Jane asked.

The question pushed him over the edge. In the next instant, his mouth was on hers—ravishing, plundering, taking everything she had to give. Jane opened and welcomed his raw sensuality. To his surprise, her hands claimed him. They were all over him, measuring the width of his shoulders—the breadth of his chest as if she wanted to know every inch of his body.

Then his mouth left hers. He dragged in much needed air. He felt Jane as she fumbled with his shirt buttons. Soon she had it open down past his chest. She was a bold one. That was the last coherent thought he had. Her hands slid inside the opening and glided through the crisp hair on his chest as she explored the hard planes of his muscles.

"Oh, Morgan," Jane moaned, awash in sensuality. She wanted him. Oh, dear heaven, how she wanted him—like a woman, not a silly girl. If she'd had the nerve to touch him like this ten years ago, she'd never have let him go.

His soft laugh broke through the haze of sensuality which blanketed her. "I guess I was right about there being something unfinished between us."

Jane froze, suddenly aware of how she was behaving. "Is this what you had in mind by unfinished business?"

"Sure. Isn't that what you thought? I'm sure you've wondered over the years how it would have been between us. We almost did it more than once but we were just kids."

Jane felt unaccountably hurt. Was sex all he had on his mind? Of course, given her behavior in the last few minutes, why should she be surprised if he thought the same about her?

"Surely you didn't think I meant anything more profound than a little weekend entertainment?" he asked, with a chuckle.

"Weekend entertainment?" she repeated in a dangerously calm voice. She'd never admit that she had wanted more than that. "Of course not." She was proud of the nonchalant tone of voice she affected. "We're both mature, as you said. Why, no one in today's world bats an eye at uncomplicated sex."

She laughed, but it was a bit shrill so she stopped. She wanted nothing more than to slap his smug face and shove him out of the swing. How dare he be so shallow!

"Morgan? Are you out here?" Penny called.

Jane shoved at Morgan in an effort to move him away from her. The porch light overhead flicked on. She shielded her eyes with her hand, praying no one would notice the twin spots of color in her cheeks.

"I need to help Amber," Jane said, thankful that Penny had saved her from making a bigger fool of herself. She jumped from the swing and ran inside as if the hounds of hell were after her.

"Let me guess," Penny said. "You were racing down memory lane, and the exertion made you warm. That's why you removed your coat and your tie and loosened your shirt."

"Penny, did anyone ever tell you that you had a smart mouth?" Morgan buttoned his shirt up except for the collar button. He took his time, using the minutes to get his emotions under control. If he did get Jane in his bed, he'd probably expire from the heat they generated. He'd never met another woman who excited him with such little effort. But what a way to go, he thought.

"So who's your friend?" Penny asked.

Morgan shrugged. "No one special."

Penny snorted. "Yeah. Right. I could see how indifferent you are to her."

He glanced at his watch. "Punctual as always. You said you planned to leave at eleven, and it's eleven on the dot. What's the matter? Did Gage bore you?"

"He was okay, but nothing to write home about."

"Come on." He rose. "Let's get the others and leave. I've got some work to do tonight." He was satisfied that Jane thought he was besotted with her. She'd think he was falling into her trap. Let her make the next move. After all, she was the one who was supposed to be doing the seducing.

Penny trailed him as he went inside to say his goodbyes. No matter how much she probed, Morgan wouldn't tell her anything about Jane.

"What's this about work? I thought we had the weekend free," she said.

Once they were in the limo, Morgan told Berk about Serena's planned arrival. He ignored Penny's surprised expression and tried to downplay the fact that he'd invited Serena.

"Why is Serena coming here?" Penny asked.

"Because I asked her to." Morgan answered with a finality in his voice that brooked no further questions.

"Who's Serena?" Carlos murmured to Penny.

"Another of Morgan's conquests," Penny said. "Serena Maria Estevez."

Carlos's eyes nearly popped out. "You mean the actress who was in the latest Bond film? Morgan knows her?"

Penny nodded. "Kind of."

"She's the most beautiful woman I've ever seen," Carlos said reverently. "Do you think I could maybe"—he blushed crimson—"maybe meet her?"

Penny smiled sweetly. "I wouldn't be a bit surprised, Carlos."

He fell back against the car seat. "Wow. That's better than anything I could imagine."

"Better than making a killing in the market?" Penny asked, looking doubtful.

"Much better," Carlos declared. Then, as if a thought occurred to him, "Is she Morgan's girlfriend?"

"Don't look so heartbroken. Serena's just a friend. She's Morgan's current official date, I guess you could say. Also, don't expect her to be like her movie image," she warned.

Penny looked thoughtful. "Morgan, I'm beginning to wonder what game you're playing."

"The only thing you need to wonder about, Penny, is whether you can be at the school by the time the alumni brunch is over tomorrow," Morgan said gruffly.

"Hey, no problem." She snapped a salute and said, "With bells on. You know. You might be right. This weekend might be entertaining after all."

Morgan frowned but didn't say anything.

"As long as I don't have to eat at the alumni brunch, I can do most anything," Penny concluded cheerfully.

"Hey, girl, some grits and fatback would put some meat on your skinny bones," Berkley called.

"Thanks, Berk, but I like my bones just the way they are."

Fifteen minutes later, Berk turned onto a gravel lane just blocks from the downtown area of Vernon. A six-foot-tall stand of pampas grass obscured the house where Berk planned to spend the night.

The limo glided through the narrow opening in the pampas grass and pulled up to the side of the house. Morgan opened the door and got out. Berkley left the engine running but popped the trunk release. Flashlight in hand, he joined Morgan. They walked to the rear of the limo where Morgan removed his suitcase.

The car door opened. "Are you sure you want to stay here?" Penny asked, looking at the darkened house that appeared a bit run-down even in the moonlight.

"I'll be fine. See you in the morning." Morgan bounded up the dozen steps leading to the high-ceilinged wraparound porch. The hinges of the screen door squealed in protest when he opened it.

"Shine the light here, Berk," he said, setting his bag down while he fumbled with the lock.

"What's going on, Morgan?" Berk asked softly.

Morgan didn't try to pretend with his friend. They'd been through too much together. The key turned stiffly in the lock. He gave Berk a condensed version of the past and the present.

"Let's just say I'm getting a little revenge," he concluded.

"You've always said it was a waste of energy to get mad or try to get even. More than once, I've heard you say that it's better to get ahead."

Morgan pushed the front door open and lifted his bag.

"Yeah, well, this time it's different."

"What's so different about this time?" Berk asked.

"This time it's personal."

Six

"Janie, it's nearly nine o'clock. You're going to miss the alumni brunch if you don't get up."

Jane groaned and pulled the pillow over her head. Maybe her mother would leave her alone. She didn't want to go to the alumni breakfast. She didn't want to go anywhere Morgan might be. After last night, she wouldn't be able to look him in the face without blushing crimson. What had possessed her? Moonlight and memories weren't enough to excuse her wanton behavior.

"Jane Louise Jones! Get your lazy rear out of bed."

This exhortation was followed by the sound of her mother's footsteps on the stairs. Then a rapping on her door that would have awakened the dead ensued.

"Enough. Enough. I'm up," Jane yelled crossly.

"Coffee's on. It'll help, dear," Brenda Jones called cheerily. "Get a move on."

Jane tossed the pillow to the floor and wondered how she and her mother could be such opposites. Brenda Jones was a perky morning person while Jane was a grumbling grouch. It usually took a hot shower and a couple of cups of coffee for her to feel like a member of the human race. Maybe she had her father's biorhythms. Wes Jones, sheriff of the parish for as long as Jane could remember, was not a morning person either. None of the deputies bothered him in the morning until after he'd had two cups of coffee.

She rubbed her temples. This morning was worse than usual. She'd tossed and turned most of the night, thanks to Morgan Sherwood. It was bad enough that he had come on to her at the party last night. And that she had yielded to his flirtation. Did he have to invade her dreams too?

Every word he'd said—every touch—had been replayed endlessly during the night. She'd had no refuge since her cursed memory insisted on going over the scene in the porch swing in excruciating detail. She'd dozed off, only to awake before dawn with her blood singing through her veins and her body clamoring for release.

Wide-eyed, Jane had stared at the ceiling until exhaustion finally claimed her about an hour before her mother shouted up the stairs.

This was so much worse than in high school because now she knew what happened between a man and a woman. Morgan had been the phantom lover caressing her with his hands, his mouth, and his body as she dreamed. Only one day of the reunion had passed, she thought, sighing. She'd be a basket case by Monday morning.

"Are you in the shower yet?" her mother shouted from downstairs.

With a long-suffering sigh, Jane climbed out of bed and headed to the bathroom. "I am now," she grumbled.

Somehow, she'd have to avoid Morgan the rest of the weekend. When she thought of how she'd all but ripped his clothes from him, she wanted to jump on the first plane to New York! Her face flooded with color. She'd just ignore him. That should send the message that she wasn't interested in some kind of overdue affair with him.

Less than an hour later, in deference to the June heat, she'd dressed in a sleeveless lime-green sheath, belted with a thin white braided leather belt. White leather cork sandals made her appear taller than her five and a half feet.

Jane descended the stairs and headed to the kitchen.

"Where's my coffee?" Jane asked, acting as if she were on her last leg, ready to collapse.

Her mother laughed and pushed a mug toward her. "I already weakened it with water and added milk and sugar."

Jane pecked her on the cheek. "Thanks, Mom. I'd never make it out the door without this."

"You drink too much coffee, dear."

"Well, it's true I probably drink more cups a day than you and Daddy, but I don't make mine nearly as strong so it probably ends up being the same amount of caffeine."

Brenda laughed. "You always were a master at rationalization."

Her words struck Jane forcefully. "Do you really think that, Mom?"

Her mother stopped what she was doing and looked

at her. "Why, Janie, of course not. I was just joking. Don't you know that?"

Jane sighed. "Sure, I knew that."

Her mother poured herself a cup of the strong black coffee and sipped it without diluting it. "Is everything all right with you this morning?"

"Of course. What could be wrong?"

"Well," Brenda paused. "You didn't have any more run-ins with Morgan, did you?"

Jane knew the color that flooded her face gave her away. Dang it!

Still she tried to convince her mother otherwise. "Of course not, Mom. In fact, Morgan and I had a very nice conversation last night." That was stretching the truth only a little. "We cleared the air, so to speak." She tried not to wince as she told that whopper.

"Good. I didn't raise you to hold grudges against other people. And I don't like having you the subject of talk in this town. Lord knows, I've had to put up with my share of it. I don't want you subjected to it also."

"Why, Mom. What do you mean?"

"That's for me to know, and you to wonder about," Brenda said tartly.

"Now, I want you to tell me the truth about what's going on between you and Morgan Sherwood."

Jane's coffee sloshed over. "Uh, what do you mean? There's nothing going on."

Brenda snorted in disbelief. "Don't try to snow me the way you do your father. I wasn't always a middle-aged housewife."

Jane looked at Brenda in surprise. "What are you trying to say?"

"Let's just say your reaction to the mere mention of his name is mighty suspicious. And when I heard what you said about him yesterday, I knew something was up. Though questioning a man's ability to, uh, please a woman is an odd way to attract his attention."

"What!" Jane stared thunderstruck at her. "I never! Where on earth did you hear that?"

"And ladies do not suggest that a man is not needed for sexual relations," Brenda continued without pause. "My goodness, self-gratification is definitely not on the list of acceptable conversation topics. Especially in this town."

"Mother! What on earth are you talking about?"

"Your remarks at school."

Jane thought back over what she'd said and decided she understood part of her mother's accusation. "All I said was that I doubt Morgan could impress me even with all his money. And I never said anything about his ability to perform—or about—" She broke off, unable to say *that* word to her mother, of all people. "About self-gratification," she finally said. "I might have said something about not needing to buy the cow to get the milk."

Brenda looked as if she were struggling with her emotions. Finally, laughter won the battle.

Jane stared at her mother, amazed that she was laughing instead of scolding. "Maybe you should have changed the gender if you wanted to use that analogy."

"That's what Morgan said," she muttered.

"Oh, he did, did he?"

"You're not mad at me?"

"No. Just be a little more prudent what you say since it will probably get distorted with repeated telling."

"It's not my fault this town is full of gossips."

"That may be, but ladies don't talk like that—unless they're among close friends. Not in Vernon."

"Mother, back when you and your friends didn't think I was paying attention, I certainly heard you discuss things worse than that. And Granny J. and that bunch of busybodies in the Ladies Club would make Howard Stern blush. Sex is the primary topic of conversation every Wednesday, not bridge."

"Let's not change the subject. We're talking about your behavior, not your grandmother's. There's already too many people who think your morals have loosened since you're living in New York City."

Privately, Jane didn't care what the townfolk thought about her morals, but she refrained from telling her mother that.

"All I'm asking is that you behave a little more circumspectly. I've never seen you act so impetuous before. Are you sure everything is okay?"

"Yes, Mom, everything's fine." Jane sighed. "I promise I'll be a perfect little Puritan from this moment on." And she wouldn't have a problem, as long as she avoided Morgan. Even in a town the size of Vernon, that shouldn't be difficult.

* * *

Less than an hour later, though, Jane realized being a model of decorum was more difficult than she'd expected.

"Jane Louise, where's your name tag?" Earleen Mushmak demanded.

"Oh, uh, I must have left it at home."

"Well, be sure and wear it tonight. It's your ticket for the prom. And what are you doing over here in the corner? You're supposed to be at Morgan's table."

"I didn't know there was assigned seating," Jane said meekly.

"Well, there is for club presidents and honors graduates. You were president of the Art Club, so you qualify. You would have known if you'd taken the trouble to read the information in your reunion packet carefully."

"I'm already seated, Miss Mushmak. I wouldn't want to leave Jason alone."

"He's supposed to be at Morgan's table too," the woman said smugly. "Did you forget he was salutatorian?"

Jane blushed. "Yes, I guess I did." She cast an apologetic glance at Jason.

"No problem, Janie. Come on. Let's go worship at the feet of the great Morgan Sherwood," Jason said with a lopsided grin.

Without making a scene, Jane didn't know how to get out of it. "Sure thing," she said brightly. "Thanks so much, Miss Mushmak," she added, unable to keep the sarcasm out of her voice.

The woman cast her a sharp glance. "You're welcome, Jane Louise." She peered at her over her glasses until Jane beat a hasty retreat.

"That woman still scares the bejeebers out of me," she grumbled to Jason.

He laughed. "I have to agree she wasn't my favorite teacher either." He took that moment to put his arm around her and hugged her close. "It's good to see you, Janie. I always thought we had something special together. I'm glad for the chance to catch up after all these years. Remember what fun we had at the senior prom?"

Jane didn't argue with Jason, but she had an entirely different view of that prom. She'd been miserable because Morgan hadn't asked her to go with him. Jason had suddenly asked at the last moment if she'd go with him. She'd agreed only because she foolishly thought it would make Morgan jealous and make him declare himself openly.

Just then she glanced at Morgan as she and Jason approached the long table set up on a raised dais. The expression on his face gave her pause. He looked as if he were furious. Then in an instant, he concealed his thoughts. Shaken, she wondered why he'd looked so angry. It wasn't her fault that she had to sit at his stupid table. He stood when they got to the dais.

"Janie and I were sent over by the mighty Mushmak," Jason said.

"Jason," Felicia, sitting on Morgan's right, squealed. "I didn't get a chance to talk with you last night."

Jane guessed that Felicia had heard Jason was newly single also. Another name for her list of eligible men.

"Felicia, you look wonderful," Jason said. Jane noticed the way his eyes moved down and then up Felicia. "Whatever you've been doing for ten years, keep on doing it." When he winked, she giggled and blushed bright red.

Jane watched the little byplay between the two. There was something insincere about Jason, she suddenly realized.

"I could say the same for you, Jason Lombardo," Felicia said. "You're like Morgan—better looking now than you were in high school. Don't you think so, Jane Louise?"

"Yes, Jason, you do look very fit." She didn't like the way he ogled Felicia. Had he looked at her that way, also?

"Well, that's high praise coming from her," Morgan, still standing, said, with a bite to his voice.

"Sherwood. How's it going?" Jason said. Jane noted that he didn't bother offering his hand to Morgan.

"Pretty good. How's it going for you?" Morgan clasped his hands behind his back as if shaking Jason's hand would be the last thing on his mind.

They'd been friends in high school, Jane recalled. What was with the way they were acting? Jane listened as Jason curtly replied to Morgan's mundane greeting.

Jason grinned, then winked at Jane. "Morgan, I see you finally put some meat on your bones. No more ninety pound weakling huh?"

"Not even close," Morgan said with a cold smile, puzzling Jane even more. Since he'd arrived in Vernon, he'd been the soul of amiability with everyone.

Except Jason. The two men obviously didn't like each other.

"You were one skinny dude in high school. No wonder you never had a date." Jason laughed, and turned to the others as if inviting the other people who had arrived and were seating themselves at the table to share the joke. A couple of women giggled, and some of the men smiled. Jane didn't find anything funny about his insulting remark. He was being obnoxious.

"As someone recently pointed out," Morgan said, "people change."

"But seldom," Jane murmured, wondering if Jason had always been such a jerk, and she'd just never noticed.

"What's that?" Jason asked, looking at her.

"Oh, nothing. I was just talking to myself," Jane said. But she could see by Morgan's eyes that he'd heard. A smile flitted across his face so quickly she wondered if she'd really seen it.

"Sit here, next to me, Jason," Felicia said, patting the chair next to her.

"Well, Janie and I were going to sit together."

"Oh, there's not another vacant seat there. Don't mind me." Jane decided she didn't want to sit next to Jason. "Go sit with Felicia. We can talk some other time."

Morgan removed the briefcase from the chair next to him and shut it, snapping the locks. "This seat is empty," he said.

"Oh, I wouldn't want to interrupt your work," Jane said.

"I was finished anyway." Morgan pulled out the chair for Jane.

She couldn't help the rush of pleasure as she settled into the chair. Briefly she felt the warmth of his fingers on the back of the chair as she leaned back. Then he moved and returned to his own chair next to her.

"Wasn't that a great party last night?" Felicia asked.

Several agreed that it was. Jane remained silent and let the conversation flow around her.

"I really enjoyed the party even if Amber's refreshments were a bit on the unhealthy side. All that fat and sugar," Felicia shuddered. "I nearly gained five pounds just looking at all that processed food."

"I never laughed so much as I did when you did your impersonation of Miss Mushmak, Felicia," Verna Wright said.

"I must have missed that," Jane said.

"Me, too," Morgan said, his eyes grazing hers.

Jane blushed. Was that when they'd been outside? Together. She knew he was thinking the same thing when she looked over at him. His eyes were on her lips. She felt a blush rise from her neck to her hairline.

She was saved by the arrival of the last people who were to sit at their table. Jane exchanged greetings with them. Once they were seated, students posing as waiters, complete with napkins over their bent arms, began serving brunch.

"What is this gelatinous goop?" Felicia asked as a plate was set in front of her.

"Brunch?" Morgan said, smiling and thanking the girl who served him.

"It looks pretty good to me," Jane said, smiling at the girl who placed a plate in front of her.

"Well, that soufflé is swimming in cheddar cheese, and I bet it's made with real cholesterol-loaded eggs. And sausage? My goodness, haven't they heard how damaging pork sausage is? I have to fight with my mom and dad every time I come visit about their horrible dietary habits. Anyone who eats fried pork must have a death wish."

Jane buttered a flaky, golden-brown biscuit. "Well, to each his own," she said, salivating at the thought of the spicy sausage. "Eating southern cooking is one of my favorite things about coming home. Try to get a homemade biscuit and sausage gravy anywhere else."

"Don't you care about your appearance?" Felicia demanded.

"Oh, I don't think Janie has to worry about her figure," Jason said. "She looks about as perfect as any woman I've seen."

Felicia's frown was a near match for Morgan's, Jane thought.

The woman didn't give up easily in her attempt to convert them. "I don't know if you should eat that soufflé. Those eggs may not be cooked all the way through. They might contain salmonella."

"I like to live dangerously," Morgan said, taking another big bite. He rolled his eyes comically. "Best salmonella I've ever had."

"Felicia," Jane said, "the Home Economics department catered this to raise money to send a delegation to a workshop at the Culinary Institute. I'm sure they went to a lot of trouble. So you might want to keep your voice down."

"If I were to eat just to avoid hurting people's feelings, I'd be as big as the side of a barn again."

Jane sighed. "The biscuits couldn't be that bad. They're delicious." She spread homemade mayhaw jelly on a piece.

"Ugh. They're made of white flour. I only eat whole wheat. Do you know what white flower does to your colon?"

"No, and I don't want to know," Morgan said, shoving a biscuit in his mouth.

Jane giggled. "One bite won't contaminate your colon, Felicia."

"Well, we could sneak out to the diner," Jason said. "They still make those wheat germ waffles. Come with me, Janie."

"The speeches should start any minute," Morgan said, glancing at his watch. "They've got everything arranged for a tour of the school. I'm sure they'd be hurt if people sneaked away."

Jane looked over at Jason. The smile seemed to have frozen on his face.

"Stay, Jason," she said, trying to smooth over the barely hidden animosity between him and Morgan.

Just then Miss Mushmak stood and walked to the podium. Her speech was filled with praise for Morgan and all he'd done for the school.

To Jane's surprise, ruddy color filled Morgan's face. He was embarrassed by her praise. After the teacher had finished, Morgan stood but stayed where he was.

He thanked his former teacher and surprised Jane by sounding sincere in his praise of the woman.

"She encouraged me at a time when no one else believed I could achieve my dreams."

Jane wanted to say that *she* had believed in him—once. When he sat again, she looked at Earleen Mushmak and saw an expression of maternal pride on the woman's face. For the first time, Jane realized that the teacher's entire life had been lived through certain special students—like Morgan—whom she'd believed could excel. The insight gave Jane a grudging respect for her.

Concentrating on her meal kept her from thinking about Morgan. When she finished eating, she lifted her coffee cup and sat back. In just a few minutes, she could make her escape.

Morgan leaned forward and whispered, "Sleep well last night?"

Jane nearly spilled her coffee. "Yes," she lied. "And you?"

"No, I tossed and turned all night," he said baldly.

"Oh. Well. I'm sorry."

"You should be. It was your fault."

"My fault? How could that be?"

He leaned closer, his blue eyes mesmerizing her. "Because you got me so hot and bothered. I couldn't stop thinking about how your hands felt on me."

Jane's eyes widened. Then she looked around to see if anyone had heard. Luckily, Felicia was talking with Verna Wright and Jason was engaged in a conversation with one of his former football buddies.

Jane shushed him. "Don't say things like that."

"Why not? It's the truth."

"Well, that doesn't mean you have to talk about it!" Jane looked around again.

He chuckled softly. "What's the matter? Afraid someone will find out about us?"

She closed her eyes, striving for patience, but that just made the picture his words had created even stronger.

"There is no us."

He reached out and stroked a lazy circle on the back of her hand. "Oh, but there is."

She watched his fingers continue to circle her hand as if they were burning the design into her flesh.

"I kept feeling your lips beneath mine."

He held her hand with both of his. His voice was so low, she had to strain to hear. "I couldn't stop wondering how your breasts would feel when I cup them in my hands."

Jane jerked her hand free. "Get out of my head," she hissed.

He leaned over and whispered in her ear. His voice was raw, hoarse with emotion. "Why should I? You've held my thoughts hostage for years."

Jane became aware that people were beginning to look at them. *Oh, Mom,* she thought. *Why is it so hard to be a good girl?*

His whisper grazed her earlobe when she turned to him. "I couldn't stop wondering how your hips would feel when I grasped them in my hands and pulled them to me."

Jane knew her face was brighter than the overhead lights. It certainly felt as if it might very well burst into flame in another moment—and so would other parts of her anatomy if she didn't get away from him.

"Ride with me today?" he asked.

"Quit saying things like that!"

"What's wrong with asking you to ride with me in the limo?"

"Oh, ride in the limo?" Jane couldn't meet his eyes.

He laughed softly. "What's the matter, Jane. Imagination getting the better of you."

"I think you'd better ride with Felicia today," Jane said, trying her best to put him beyond reach.

"No. I don't think you want me and Felicia together in the back of the limo. She might take advantage of me."

"Is that what you plan to do to me?" Jane asked, breathless.

Morgan considered her question. He had to hand it to her. She certainly played a subtle game of seduction. How had she maneuvered him into taking the active role again in this bewitchment?

"I won't take anything from you that you don't want to give," he finally said. "I'm not the kind of man who takes what he wants. When we make love, you'll see I'm just a man at the mercy of his desire."

Jane sucked in her breath. "You're mad. We're not going to make love."

"Are you sure about that? Haven't you thought about it? Fantasized about you and me? Doing what we didn't do ten years ago?"

"This has to stop," Jane said, desperation in her voice. Her voice rose. "You're being very insulting with your smirks and your condescending attitude."

People up and down the table giggled. When she realized that she'd been more forceful than necessary, she favored him with a nasty look.

Morgan grinned. "You're awfully appealing when you blush. You look like a textbook illustration of hot and bothered."

"You absolutely bring out the worst in me."

"With you, that's not difficult to do," he said.

Felicia giggled and leaned toward Morgan. "This is going to be such a fun day. Janie, did Morgan tell you he arranged for a fleet of limousines to take everyone on the tour of the town?"

Jane smiled with false sweetness. "No, he didn't. Isn't that wonderful?"

"You'll have to ride with Morgan and me," Felicia said. "You too, Jason."

"Oh, no. I think that's not necessary. I've got my mom's Chevy. I'll just poke along in it," Jane said.

"Now, Jane Louise. Don't be such a stick-in-the-mud," Felicia said. "Make her say yes, Jason. It'll be an all day party. What could be more fun?"

Riding a donkey from Louisiana to New York for fun was right up there with riding in Morgan's limo, Jane thought rebelliously.

"Sure, Janie will go," Jason said, winking at her.

Before Jane could say that Jason didn't have the right to speak for her, Felicia jumped in again. "Good. It's settled then. We'll spend the day together."

The student waiters cleared the tables, and the principal rose to make his speech. He talked about the improvements to the school that were planned for next year and the generosity of an unknown benefactor in donating money for a new library.

Jane knew that had to be Morgan again. He was the only alumnus with the means and the inclination to do something like that.

"That's very generous of you," she said.

"I don't know what you mean," he said, again acting as if he were embarrassed by recognition of his generosity.

There were more facets to the man than she had ever suspected. What else about Morgan didn't she know?

Seven

"All right, children, form groups of twenty," Earleen Mushmak directed from the podium. "Morgan, you and your party in the first group." She beamed at him. "Thirty minutes after the first group leaves, the second group may go."

"Shall we go, ladies?" Morgan took Jane's arm in his left hand and Felicia's in his right. Short of making a scene, Jane could not free herself.

"I don't need your assistance," Jane protested.

"I wouldn't think of leaving you ladies unescorted."

"Hey, wait a minute," Jason called.

"I must ask you to form a column two across," the senior girl assigned as their guide stated. "Miss Mushmak said you had to walk this way." Her earnest manner amused Jane and reminded her of herself when she'd been a student.

"Keep your hands and your objects to yourself," Felicia cracked, reciting the number one rule they'd heard expressed in every class from kindergarten to high school. Everyone laughed.

Jane's amusement dimmed when she realized Morgan had paired himself with her for the tour. She looked back and saw Jason charming a very susceptible Felicia. She decided not to interrupt them.

They started down the hallway. Their guide pointed out the trophy case that held the one football state trophy and the numerous band trophies and scholastic medals students had won over the years. Vernon High had never had much of an athletic program, but the band had been one of the best in the state, and the students could compete scholastically with any larger school.

Next came the offices, then the new computer lab built within the last year. Was this another example of Morgan's benevolence toward his alma mater? Jane glanced over at him.

After they peeked into several classrooms, they were led to the music wing that held the band hall and the choir room.

"Oh, dear, it's dark in here," their guide said. They could hear her hands scrambling along the wall as she searched for the light switches.

Jane felt her arm jerked as Morgan pulled her quickly down a short hall and into a pitch-black practice room.

"What are you doing?" she whispered in alarm.

He backed her against the wall. His arms braced on either side of her head, effectively imprisoning her. Jane could have told him he didn't need to hold her in place. The strength of his desire did that.

"I'm yielding to insanity," he muttered.

"What?" she quavered. When his head lowered to hers, there was no doubt in her mind what he was doing.

The kiss was endless—soft and drugging, then demanding. It went on and on, draining her of resistance and filling her with desire. Then his mouth slid to her throat. He bit the tender flesh there and made her knees shake.

"Say you'll meet me tonight," he demanded, his voice hot against her skin.

Jane couldn't talk. She couldn't even think. He pressed against her. She moaned. His body was large and hard-muscled. Of course, that wasn't all that was rock solid about him, she thought, clinging to him to keep from falling.

He made her feel desires she'd never known before. Up until now, her love life had been fairly tame and commonplace. He made her want to be wild and daring.

She felt the bricks of the wall pressing into her as he sought her lips again. She didn't hesitate. Though part of her—the sane, logical part—said to resist. To run. To put distance between them because that might cool the heat that flared between them each time they met.

They kissed. And then they kissed some more. Jane concentrated on showing him all she'd learned about the art in ten years. Dazed, she realized that he'd learned something too in their years apart—how to drive her mad with desire.

"Come on, Jane, say you'll meet me."

"Good girls don't do things like that." The words, spoken in a breathless, teasing voice, tumbled out as if of their own volition.

He froze. His breathing was harsh in the tiny, dark room. That's what she'd told him all those years ago.

"Maybe you're not so good?" That's what he'd said when she'd climbed into his car that first time when they'd met late at Dairy Palace.

"I'm worse than that. I'm beginning to think I'm the original bad girl."

"You know what Mae West said, don't you?" he teased. She heard the smile in his voice and felt it as his lips touched hers with butterfly kisses.

"No, what?"

"When she was good she was very, very good. But when she was bad, she was better."

Jane couldn't help but laugh softly and rub against him, rotating her hips. She burned and she wanted him to burn too.

"Come on. Be bad with me, Jane. You know you want to. Meet me tonight. The usual place."

His lips slid down her throat, down to her neckline. She felt his tongue teasing her skin above the fabric. Then his fingers traced where he'd placed the wet kisses, spreading fire and desire. Then, slowly, his fingers skimmed below the neckline, tracing the curves that swelled above the lacy cups of her bra. She wondered if he could hear the hammering of her heart.

"I won't let you rejoin the others until you promise," he vowed. "They'll come looking for us any moment."

"Yes," she whispered, not needing any coercion. "I promise."

"Good." He straightened and tugged on the sides of her dress. "Come on." Calmly he pulled her through the doorway. Their group was just coming out of the music room.

Panicked, Jane brushed her hands down her dress and fluffed her short crop of curls. She hoped she didn't look as disheveled as she felt. When some in their group glanced her way, she saw them snicker.

Stricken, she looked up at Morgan. Hastily her thumb raised to wipe her lipstick from his mouth.

"Oh." He flushed and pulled his handkerchief from his back pocket. He turned his back, wiped his mouth, then passed the red-streaked linen to her.

"Sorry," he said, sounding as if he meant it.

"So what happened to you two?" Jason asked curtly, walking toward them. Bemused, Jane watched Felicia follow him.

"Nothing. Jane thought she'd lost an earring so I helped her look for it," Morgan said coolly.

"You must have lost them both since you don't have any earrings on," Felicia said. "Too bad." She claimed Morgan's arm. "Come on. Let's rejoin the others."

Jane ignored the twinge of jealousy at seeing the woman clasp his arm to her breasts. She walked next to Jason. When he tried to take her hand, she pulled free.

After their tour was over, Jane's plan to escape in her mom's car was neatly derailed by Jason. She felt as if she were in some kind of soap opera plot, cast between the two men with Felicia as a rival.

"Come on. Penny and Berk are waiting for us," Morgan said, ushering them outside where a line of limousines waited in the school bus loading zone.

A small crowd of townspeople had gathered to take

a firsthand look at the unusual caravan. Someone was taking pictures. Jane guessed it must be for the weekly paper. This was certainly an event that would live in town lore for years to come, she thought, gazing at the dozen black stretch limousines.

At Morgan's limo, the only white one there, he introduced Berkley to her. "I think you met Penny Tranh, my administrative assistant, last night?" he said, lips twitching.

"Yes. Nice to see you again," Jane murmured, striving for a nonchalance she didn't feel.

Penny nodded. "Likewise." Then she claimed Morgan for a private chat.

Berkley exchanged pleasantries with Jane, then excused himself when Verna Wright dashed up.

"Hey, Verna," Jane called, glad to see a friendly face.

Verna turned and reluctantly, it seemed to Jane, walked around to where she, Felicia, and Jason stood.

"Are you riding with us?" Jane asked.

Verna's eyes shone. "Well, kind of. I'll talk to you later, Janie. My date is waiting." She went back to Berkley who held the door open while she slid across the driver's seat to the middle of the bench seat.

"Oh!" Jane said, smiling.

"They make a good-looking couple, don't they?" Morgan asked quietly.

She hadn't heard him come back. "Yes, they do."

"It's odd you and your chauffeur act more like friends than employer and employee," Felicia said.

"You think so?" Morgan asked.

"Yes. Doesn't your driver wear one of those chauffeur hats?" Felicia asked, as she stepped into the car.

Morgan grinned. "No, he doesn't, but the thought of him wearing one is mighty entertaining. Maybe I should get him one. What do you think, Penny?"

"I think you must have a death wish," Penny said, stepping aside so Jason could enter the limo. He took the facing seat since Felicia had settled into the regular seat.

Jane prepared to step up, but Morgan restrained her. "Just a minute, someone else is joining us."

"Who?" she asked turning to look at him.

"Janie! Wait for me."

"Amber! I didn't think you were going to be able to make the town tour," Jane said, smiling at her friend with relief. Amber's presence ought to ease some of the tension.

Amber climbed in and settled on the backseat next to Felicia.

Jane looked inside. She wanted to sit next to Amber, but she knew the remaining seat there was for Morgan.

"Excuse me," Penny said, stepping in front of her and climbing into the rear of the limo. "Sorry, folks, but you're going to have to move around. I can't ride backward. It makes me carsick."

"No problem," Amber said, scrambling to the backward seat next to Jason.

"Your secretary is joining us, Morgan?" Felicia asked.

"She's not my secretary, Felicia."

"I'm his administrative assistant, Ms. Banks. And, yes, Morgan convinced me the town tour might be interesting. Also, we have some business to attend to. This will give me a few minutes out of his oh-so-busy day," she said. Her smile did nothing to alleviate the sarcastic tone in her voice.

Felicia patted the spot next to her. "Come on, Morgan, here's your seat."

"Oh, Felicia, I'm sorry, but Jane has an inner-ear problem," Amber said. "She gets dizzy if she rides backward. She'll have to sit on the backseat with Penny and Morgan."

Jane gaped at Amber. Why, she was in this scheme with Morgan. "Uh, that's okay. I might be able to risk it for the short drive." She glared at Amber.

"No, Jane Louise," Felicia said, quickly moving to the other seat. "I'll sit here so Morgan can gaze on my gorgeousness," she quipped.

"What about me, Felicia," Jason said, throwing his arm around her. "Blind me with your beauty, you sexy thing."

Felicia giggled and snuggled close to him. Jane wondered if she was not interested in Morgan so much as in a man's attention—any man. Low self-esteem did that to some women, and Felicia had possessed the lowest in high school she'd ever seen.

Morgan settled into the seat next to Penny and motioned for Jane to be seated. Trapped, she silently sat next to him.

"Okay, Berk," Morgan called. "Nursing home first, and don't break any speed limits. We wouldn't want Jane's father to pull us over."

Penny giggled. "Berk will make you pay for that."

Jane wondered again about Morgan's relationship with his people. It was definitely different.

"Is your dad really the sheriff?" Penny asked.

When Jane nodded, Penny said, "That must have been tough."

"You don't know the half of it," Amber said. "Jane never had the luxury of getting in trouble. She and her sisters were the models for good behavior the rest of us hellions were supposed to imitate."

A smoked glass partition slid shut, closing the driver's compartment off from the rest of the car.

"Berk must want privacy," Penny murmured.

Jane had feared that Morgan would embarrass her with his attention, but he talked with Penny on the way to the nursing home, which, she thought, was a weird place to begin a tour of the town.

Penny opened a compartment on the side and pulled out a sheaf of papers. Jane noticed they were faxes.

Morgan quickly went through them. He was fast and decisive as he told her what to do with each one. Despite the situation, she found herself admiring his keen mind. She wondered exactly what he had done to make his fortune. Maybe she'd have a chance to ask him.

When they pulled into the nursing home, she noticed that none of the other limos had followed them. Morgan led the way inside. To her surprise, he was greeted by name by Mrs. Myerson, one of her mother's friends.

Jane nodded and smiled as Mrs. Myerson gave a short speech describing their facility. Then she led the way to what she termed their pride and joy.

Down the hall, past the front parlor, Mrs. Myerson led them into a large room with a piano at one end.

At the other end was a U-shaped set-up with computers, monitors, and printers. At each computer sat an elderly nursing home resident. Some had a young aide sitting next to them.

"What is this?" Jane asked, looking around.

"This is our computer lab. Some geriatric specialists in California have noted computers enrich the lives of the elderly. Using them helps overcome the plagues of old age—boredom, loneliness, isolation, and mental decline. Learning to use e-mail and the Internet can be a lifeline to the rest of the world for people who are isolated." Her smile faded. "And there's often no one more isolated than a nursing home resident, especially when children and grandchildren live far away. This is a way for them to reconnect with relatives and old friends."

"That's nice," Jason said, checking his watch. "Shouldn't we be moving along? We're supposed to go to that new restaurant for lunch."

Amber cast a withering glance at him. "Mrs. Myerson has been organizing experienced volunteers to act as tutors for the residents who are interested in learning how to use the computers."

"Amber was one of the first to volunteer, and she helped organize the others. The response to the computer lab kind of surprised us."

"I thought the other computers we ordered would have been delivered by now," Penny said, frowning.

"Oh, they have been, but we haven't got the tables yet to set them up. The freight company said they should arrive in a couple of days."

Jane looked at Morgan. He'd done this, too. At least

he was the kind of successful entrepreneur who believed in spreading his wealth around.

"I think I'll go wait in the car if you don't mind," Felicia said. "All these old people are just too depressing."

"Yeah, I'll wait with you," Jason said.

"I'm surprised by their attitude," Amber muttered.

"Now, dear, not everyone feels comfortable in a nursing home environment. We can't condemn those who don't have the emotional resources to relate to the elderly in a positive way," Mrs. Myerson said.

Jane walked over to the people at the computers. They were intent on their tasks.

One white-haired lady who appeared to be the oldest caught her attention.

"Excuse me," she said.

The woman looked up. Her faded hazel eyes looked away from the e-mail she was painstakingly typing with swollen fingers obviously twisted by arthritis. Her face lit up. "Janie! Janie Jones, it is you."

"Yes, Mrs. Luce. It's wonderful to see you again." Jane hugged her former piano teacher. "I didn't know you were living here now."

"Yes, dear. I just couldn't manage that big old house any longer. My older sister Evelyn lost her husband last year so we decided to move in here together."

They chatted a few minutes, then Morgan walked over. He smiled and gently shook the elderly woman's hand when Jane introduced them. "I see you're composing a message, Mrs. Luce," he said.

"Yes. I'm writing to my great-grandson who lives in Florida. He's such a dear boy. I haven't seen him since he was a baby. His mother, bless her heart, has been a single parent until recently. They've never been able to afford the expenses of travel."

"Does he have a computer at home?" Jane asked.

"His mother's new husband has one. It took me a while to learn how to work these things, but once I did, I wrote my granddaughter and gave her my e-mail address. She sends me messages from her office usually, but Teddy e-mails me practically every day. Sometimes it's just a line or two, but it's so nice. Every day I can come in here and check my e-mail. They sent me an electronic bouquet of flowers for Mother's Day."

Jane listened to Morgan talk with Mrs. Luce. She looked around the warm yellow walls with oversized prints on the wall depicting American scenes from decades ago. Modern life had brought about staggering change for her grandmother's generation. Jane was glad some of the changes, like these computers, were positive.

A short while later, they left Mrs. Luce and the others to their Internet surfing and followed Mrs. Myerson as she gave them a tour of the rest of the nursing home. It was scrupulously clean and the staff was smiling and friendly.

Morgan talked to Penny in a low voice. Penny nodded occasionally and offered some comments.

There was much more to Morgan Sherwood than Jane had suspected. A lot of people would have left a small town like Vernon and never looked back, but Morgan hadn't. He'd remembered the place and its needs and had tried to do something about it. Knowing that, Jane was filled with pride for him and for his accomplishments.

He made it easy for her to overlook his past behavior as the actions of an insecure teenager, and he made it difficult for her to remember that she didn't love him anymore.

She didn't, did she?

Eight

The sun was just sinking below the horizon when Jane arrived at the school for the dinner dance. The auditorium was decorated with crepe paper streamers, giant paper flowers, and accordion-pleated tissue paper bells, just like a high school prom—from the forties, maybe. Even the music sounded like something from a couple of generations back.

She laughed as she recognized swing tunes from the Buddy Rich orchestra. Without being told, she knew which civic organization had sponsored tonight's dance for the reunion class.

Sure enough, when she looked around, she saw her grandmother surrounded by her friends from the Vernon Ladies Bridge Club. Shaking her head in amusement, she walked over.

"Hello, Granny J. Good evening, ladies."

"Janie, what do you think about the decorations?" Granny J. asked.

"They're certainly different," Jane said, smiling.

"The ladies and I thought recreating our own senior prom might be kind of fun. Show you young people how we did things before plastic was invented," her grandmother said.

"We even found a deejay who agreed to play some of the tunes mixed in with your kind of music, dear," Mamie Holt chirped.

"Miss Mamie, it's nice to see you," Jane said. The dear old lady still wore enough makeup for two women. She'd never given up the false eyelashes that looked like two drunk caterpillars asleep on her eyelids. "I hope you rode over here with someone tonight instead of driving?"

To her relief, the woman said, "Oh my, yes, Janie. I limit my driving to the daylight hours since your daddy made them take away my license." She fluttered her eyelashes in outrage.

Jane thought it better not to comment.

One of the other ladies said, "I remember dancing to this the night my Bobby proposed to me."

"Yes, you could really shake a leg, Patty," Granny J. said. "You beat me and Herman out of first place in the jitterbug contest. Oh, but my Herman could dance." She sighed wistfully.

Jane impulsively hugged her grandmother. She had no trouble envisioning her irrepressible grandmother out doing the jitterbug. After all, she's the one who had taught Jane the dance, along with a few others from that era.

"Ladies, if you'll excuse me, I'll find my table now. Thank you for going to such trouble on our behalf." Jane walked to the tables arranged on the far side of the room.

Gold cloths and a votive candle centerpiece transformed the lunchroom tables into a cozy setting. Well,

Jane mused, at least as cozy as a high school lunch-room could be.

The music changed to a more modern song—one from the sixties. Jane smiled and hummed along with the Beatles. She waved at Amber when she saw her come through the double doors.

"How do you like it?" Jane spread her arms wide. She felt carefree and unaccountably happy.

"It's magnificent." Amber clapped her hands in delight. "I half expect my grandparents to glide across the floor."

"Well, they may make it yet. The night is young," Jane said.

"Oh, Janie, I love your dress!" Amber touched the narrow white pleats of the dress that seemed shaped to Jane's body. "Is it a real Fortuny?" she asked in awe.

"Oh, no. I could never afford a real one. This is a reproduction a friend of mine made for me."

"It's beautiful. It makes me feel like a country bumpkin in my movie star knock-off."

"Hey, don't sell yourself short, Amber. That pink silk looks better on you than it ever did on Gwyneth Paltrow."

Amber twirled, sending her ballgown skirt belling around her. "You really think so?"

Jane nodded. "Where's Steve?"

"Parking the car."

"Before he gets here, I've got a little bone to pick with you. Why are you conspiring with Morgan to throw me at him?"

Amber laughed. "Oh, that." She shrugged. "It seemed like a good idea at the time. I was just sick of

Felicia and her attitude." She looked around. "Oh, there's Steve. And look who followed him in," she added, grinning impishly.

Jane felt a moment of panic when she saw Morgan. She wished she'd checked her makeup and hair when she'd first arrived.

"Don't let him see you watching him," Amber said, "you look way too anxious."

Jane quickly turned around, then felt ridiculous for following Amber's silly advice.

She jumped when Steve put his hand on her shoulder. "Hey, girls," he said. He leaned down and kissed Amber on the lips. Then he handed her a corsage box.

"Oh, Steve," Amber said softly.

Jane watched enviously as he pulled the baby pink roses from the clear box and slipped it on Amber's wrist. The tiny corsage was perfect. Amber had it all—a beautiful child, happy domesticity, a gorgeous husband who thought she was the greatest.

What did she have? Jane thought wistfully. A career in New York wasn't the same as a loving husband in your bed each night.

She could sense Morgan before he said anything. He slipped his arm around her waist and pulled her close. "I would have brought you flowers," he murmured, "but they would have detracted from your beauty."

"That sounds suspiciously like a compliment."

"If there's any doubt in your mind, then I must need practice."

"I think you're pretty practiced as it is."

He quirked a brow. "Does that mean I sound insincere? If so, I really need to work on my wooing skills."

"Is that what you're doing?" Jane asked softly, eyes dropping. "Wooing me?"

Morgan sidled closer. In a husky voice, he said, "I think that's what we're both doing, isn't it?"

She was so beautiful in the unusual dress that it nearly hurt him to look at her. He felt odd, as if he might shrivel up and die if he couldn't touch her—couldn't make love to her.

To hell with her plan to seduce him and then kick him out of her life. Jane Louise Jones was in for quite a surprise because he wasn't going anywhere. If she slept with him, then she was his. For keeps. He'd do whatever it took to win her. If it meant keeping her in a sensual fog, then he was more than willing to do that.

All he wanted was her next to him each night. If she'd marry him, he'd take her in a New York minute. He had enough love for both of them. Maybe in time, she'd come to love him too. Who was he kidding? He'd loved her when he was eighteen, and he still loved her.

"I've never seen a woman as beautiful as you," he said softly. He could have added that he'd never wanted another woman with such intensity.

Jane looked up. She started to return the compliment, but she saw Penny, Berk, Verna, and Carlos heading toward them. There was to be no privacy for the evening, it seemed. Morgan's entourage was most unwelcome right then.

"Hey, you guys clean up real good," Morgan said.

"Careful with those compliments, Morgan, you might turn my head," Penny drawled, flicking a piece of imaginary lint from the red silk halter evening gown.

The deejay switched from the Beatles to Bill Haley and the Comets.

"Where'd they find this deejay?" Penny asked.

"Go ask the Ladies Bridge Club," Jane said, inspired. She pointed to the group of white and blue-haired women in the corner.

"Bridge Club?" Penny asked, her dark eyes sparkling. "I love bridge. I think I will go chat with the ladies."

"What's the joke?" Morgan asked when Jane and Amber burst into laughter.

"Nothing," Jane said.

"Nothing," Amber said. "The ladies of the Bridge Club will take good care of your friend." She looked at Jane, and Jane looked at her. Then they laughed again.

"You girls are so bad," Verna said, giggling.

"What is the joke, Verna?" Berk asked, a proprietary arm at her waist. When she kept giggling with the other two women, Berk looked at Morgan, perplexed.

Morgan shook his head. "There must be something in the water here."

"Take my word for it," Steve said. "There is. Get out while you can."

Morgan eyed Jane. "No, I think I'll stick around and take my chances."

Jane smiled with pleasure. When the deejay

changed to a Benny Goodman song, Steve suggested they find a table and sit.

"It might be a while before something our generation can dance to is played," he said.

"Good idea," Morgan said. A lone couple on the dance floor caught his eye. "Look, it's Penny."

"I didn't know she could do that kind of dance," Carlos said. "What do you call that?"

"It's a fox trot," Jane said. "But who is that she's dancing with?"

"Oh, that's Les from the fertilizer plant," Steve said. "I'd never have suspected he could dance. Of course, he's old enough to remember that song from his youth."

They watched in silence as the gray-haired man and dark-haired Penny moved around the floor. They looked good together.

Amber choked back a laugh. "And he's single." She elbowed Jane.

"Oh, no," Jane moaned, looking toward her grandmother's group. The women each had a man collared and were talking earnestly to their victims.

"You don't get entertainment like this in New York City, I bet," Amber said, snickering.

"What?" Morgan asked, frowning, as he followed their line of sight.

"Yoohoo! Morgan!" The painfully cheerful voice rang out.

Jane groaned. "It's Felicia." Why couldn't the woman have met a single guy in Houston? Surely there was someone in that city she could have sunk her fake nails into. Did she have to come husband hunting here?

"Let's sit down," Amber said, shooing them over to a table. Amber's attempt to get them seated before Felicia strutted over amused Jane, but she appreciated it deeply.

The group took the table nearest the dance floor. Steve and Amber sat with Jane and Morgan across from them. Berk and Verna sat together at the end of the table and held hands. They seemed to be so wrapped up in each other that they didn't hear anything except the soft words they exchanged. Jane was amazed at their intimacy, since they'd known each other such a short time.

Felicia had gone all out, wearing a black strapless bustier that left little to the imagination. A slit up the side of the dress reached her upper thigh. It was a gorgeous dress, and Jane had to admit Felicia carried it off well.

Felicia looked miffed because there was no free space for her to sit next to Morgan since Carlos had quickly filled that seat. She settled for the chair next to Carlos.

Then Jason arrived. He threw sour looks at the others and sank onto the chair next to Felicia. He seemed to sulk for a good five minutes.

Morgan regaled them all with some of his exploits on Wall Street. Jane tried to ignore the snide remarks Jason sprinkled throughout Morgan's anecdotes.

In a self-deprecating manner, Morgan told of the funny mistakes he'd made on his climb to success. He took pains to draw Carlos and Berk into the conversation, though Berk seemed more than willing to talk only to Verna.

During a lull in the conversation, the music—something from the acid rock generation—became too loud for cross-table conversation, but not too loud for Penny who was dancing with a guy younger than she. Jane turned to Morgan and said, "Tell me about Berkley."

"There's not much to tell. He and I roomed together in college. He wanted to go into government service. I wanted to make money. We both got what we wanted."

"How did he get from government service to personal bodyguard?"

Morgan shrugged. "It's just a temporary thing. I suspect he's found himself again." Morgan smiled when he saw Berk lean over and kiss Verna.

"Was he lost?"

"Yeah. He was." He told her how Berk's fiancée had been killed in a car wreck and how Berk had nearly drowned in grief.

"So you pulled him out of the bottle and gave him something to focus on other than his loss."

"No, he pulled himself out. I just happened to be there when he got it together and stayed sober."

"You know, you're a very nice man, Morgan."

Morgan looked uncomfortable, which didn't surprise her.

"What's going to happen to him now?"

"He'll be moving on, though I wish he'd seriously consider my offer to handle security for the company."

"Maybe he will. He seems to have really fallen for Verna."

"You don't know the half of it. He's already proposed."

"What? That's insane."

"Why? If you feel it's right, then it probably is," he said.

"But they just met!"

"Time doesn't mean anything if you're in love. Ten minutes can feel like ten years, and ten years can feel like ten minutes."

Jane stared at him. She took a deep breath and asked, "Are we still talking about Berk and Verna?"

"What do you think?"

The noise seemed to fade as she looked deep into his eyes. What she saw there made her heart beat even faster.

"I think I'm ready to find out what I missed ten years ago."

Morgan smiled and reached for her hand. He lifted it, turned her hand, palm up, and burned a kiss onto the tender skin there.

Her fingers curled—and so did her toes. Jane smiled mistily. She wanted to leave with him right then.

"Hey, look who Penny's dancing with now," Steve yelled.

Jane's gaze never dropped from Morgan's. His blue eyes promised and she accepted that wordless promise.

"Come on. The deejay's playing the Village People," Felicia yelled, jumping up and tugging Jason's hand.

"Come on, Janie," Amber yelled, pulling her husband along with her.

The intensity around Jane and Morgan dissipated. He grinned at her. "Do you YMCA?"

She grinned happily. "Sure. Why not?"

On the dance floor, she noticed that her grandmother and the Bridge Club were dancing to the YMCA song. She laughed. The ladies even knew the hand movements.

Penny suddenly was next to them. "Morgan, you've got to rescue me from those maniacs," she gasped.

"What do you mean?" he yelled over the music. "What maniacs?"

"Those women! They've still got half a dozen single guys lined up to dance with me," Penny said, sounding rather desperate.

Jane's laughter pealed. "Don't fight it, Penny. It'll only get worse if you do."

Penny looked at her. "Can't you call them off?"

"Nope. No force on earth can stop the matchmaking power of those ladies," Jane said cheerfully.

Morgan laughed. "Just say no, Penny."

She favored him with a dark look. "That's easy for you to say. I think you've already got a plan to get out of their trap," she muttered.

Morgan didn't appear to hear Penny's complaint, but Jane did. Uneasily, she wondered what Penny meant.

When the interactive, high-energy song ended, a

slow sensuous beat began. The mellow voice of Sade floated through the auditorium.

Morgan held his arms in the classic posture and asked, "Dance with me?"

Jane thrilled to the look in his eyes. They'd never had a chance to dance together, in each other's arms, before. She forced Penny's odd statement from her mind and stepped into his embrace. She wouldn't allow anything to ruin this evening.

Slowly, sensuously, Morgan led her in the steps of a rhumba. He pulled her closer. She could feel him— hot and hard against her abdomen. She could hardly breathe. She seemed to be one big pounding pulse point. With a sigh of capitulation, she relaxed against him and welcomed his maleness. She closed her eyes, wanting to block out everything except Morgan and the way he made her feel.

Then Morgan stopped moving. "Pardon me, but I'm cutting in," Jane heard Jason say.

Morgan's eyes were cold as he reluctantly released her.

Disappointed, Jane went into Jason's arms. When he tried to pull her close, she resisted.

He chuckled. "No up close and personal with me? Is that reserved for your buddy, Morgan?"

"I'd like to look at you when we dance," she said by way of explanation.

He chuckled, and they talked of the reunion and the softball game that was to take place tomorrow afternoon.

"The reunion has been more fun than I thought it would be," Jane said.

When the dance was over, they sat down. Felicia was trying to get Morgan to dance, but he said he and Penny had to discuss business. So she turned to Jason instead.

As soon as the next slow dance came on, he looked at Jane.

"Now it's our turn."

"Yes," Jane agreed, heart hammering. Her face glowed with pleasure.

Being in his arms was heaven. He was a man who could dance—every woman's secret dream—but more importantly, he fit next to her as if he'd been created just for her.

"Remember your promise this morning?" he asked, his lips close to her ear.

"What promise?" she asked, coquettishly, smiling into his eyes.

"Tease." He chuckled and kissed the soft auburn curls. "You promised to meet me tonight."

"That was a promise made under duress."

"A man has to use the weapons at his disposal."

"Like a dark practice room and a kiss that steals your breath away?"

"Is that what my kisses do to you?"

"Among other things," she said with a sexy smile that drew a low groan from him.

"You're killing me," Morgan said, his arms tightening. "Say you'll be there."

"Where?" Jane parried. Her hands pulled free from his dance embrace to encircle his neck. Her fingers teased the dark hair at the base of his neck.

"Our place," he whispered.

"Are you going to park behind the Dairy Palace in that big old limo? I think that would attract quite a bit of attention, don't you? We might as well take out a full page ad in the weekly paper that we're going to go make out after the dance."

"I thought we might do more than make out this time," he said quietly. His eyes searched hers.

"Whew! You sure know how to make a girl nervous." Jane bit her lower lip. "I don't know. It's one thing to be spontaneous and impulsive. It's another thing to stand on the dance floor and agree to . . . to . . ." She wanted to say *make love,* but then she decided not to. "To have sex with you."

"Forewarned is forearmed," he said, coming to a halt even though the music still played. "I'll make it easy for you, Jane. No more games. If you show up, it means you want everything I want. If you don't"—he shrugged—"then you don't. It's as easy as that. You've had ten years to make this decision. I'll wait until midnight."

Nine

She wasn't coming. Morgan checked his watch for the hundredth time. Why had he made it sound like an ultimatum? He was an idiot! What if he had scared her off?

He was startled by the headlights of an approaching car. He held his breath, then released it with a sigh of relief when he recognized the Chevy Jane had been driving. He felt nearly dizzy with relief.

She pulled up next to him and rolled down her window.

Her smile made everything all right.

He smiled back, feeling as if he wanted to embrace the whole world.

"Hi," he said.

"Hi. Where's the limo?"

"I decided you were right. It might be a bit conspicuous. Besides, Berk needed it so he rented this car for me."

Neither said anything for several seconds.

Then Morgan started the car. "Follow me," he said.

Jane hesitated only a moment. "All right." She let him pull out before she circled around the open space and followed him. To her surprise, he led her to his grandmother's house. She hadn't known he still owned it.

She gave only a passing thought to propriety then willed herself to accept whatever consequences arose. Parking behind his car in the narrow drive, she cut the lights and opened the car door.

This was it. She'd waited ten years for him.

Before she could get cold feet, Morgan was beside her. His mouth captured hers in a kiss that swept away all doubts and fears. Jane pressed against him and felt his heart beating as strong and hard as hers. She felt the sting of tears because she'd waited so long for him, and she loved him so much.

Her eyes fluttered. Loved him? She searched her mind and her heart. Yes, loved him, she decided, re-signed to the idea.

Then he broke the kiss. He simply held her while he tried to get his breathing under control. "This is your last chance to back out," he said, his voice harsh and ragged.

Jane shook her head. "No, this is what I want. You are what I want."

"You sound as if you really mean that," he said.

"Do you doubt me?" She pressed against him, feel-ing a sudden chill. "I want you so much I would have made love with you in the car," she vowed.

"No. Not in a car." His fingers traced her jaw line then lifted her chin so that she had to look into his eyes. "I want to be in bed with you. Like lovers."

She linked her arm with his. "Then let's find our bed, Morgan."

He walked with her to the front of the house. Moonlight silvered the azaleas and lit the way up the steps to the front porch. The screen door squawked loudly in the night. Morgan inserted the key and turned it then nudged the door open with his foot. He turned to Jane and lifted her into his arms and carried her into the house.

Jane closed her eyes and looped her arms about his neck. She lay her head against his chest and treasured each second of this time together.

Morgan turned on no lights as he made his way through the darkness to a room in the back. When he finally stopped and lowered her, Jane felt the bed beneath her. Her hands reached out on either side to steady herself.

For a moment, she felt afraid and uncertain, but only for a moment.

"It's all right," Morgan said, gentling her as his hands stroked down her arms. He sat beside her on the bed and kissed her cheek, then the corner of her eye, then the curve of her ear.

He continued this way, as if he knew she needed to be reassured that he would treasure the gift she was about to bestow on him. Finally, it was Jane who sought his mouth.

Morgan kissed her as if it were his sole purpose in living.

"Please," Jane moaned, reaching for his hands. She placed them on the bodice of her dress and that was all the encouragement he needed.

"This is the most beautiful dress I've ever seen," he whispered. "But I'd like it even better draped on the chair over there."

The sound of her zipper was loud in the dark. Jane felt the dress slide off her shoulders as if by magic. The same magic made her lingerie and his clothes vanish minutes later.

Then she was clasped to him. Every inch of her skin was sensitized to the delicious warmth of his body. Nothing could feel better than the sensual languor that stole through her body. Then he showed her the real magic.

His hands, his mouth, his body—all conspired to assault her senses until she was panting and begging.

"Morgan, please," she moaned, jerking in his arms. "Now, please. I want you."

"Your slightest wish is my command," he said, giving himself to her completely.

Jane cried out. Their lovemaking was the kind she'd only read about—but never experienced. Somehow, she'd always known it would be this way with him.

"Morgan," she gasped.

"Yes, love?" he asked. His arms shook with strain, but he never ceased his rhythm. He pushed her higher and farther than she'd ever been before. Then, she fell over the edge to the other side of desire, his name on her lips when she cried out. Tears sprang to her eyes as she held him close. She could never let him go now. He was hers.

A short while later, Jane trailed kisses down his throat. Her tongue tasted his skin. "You're salty," she said, smiling.

He returned the favor, sucking at the tender cord of her neck. "So are you."

"Tell me what happened after you left town?" she

asked, settling for that question instead of the one she wanted to ask.

He told her of his scholarship years at Harvard and how he'd begun his company. He made light of the difficult time and the struggles he'd endured. With a smile, he told of how he'd brought Penny, and then Carlos, into the company.

"Had you become successful before your grandmother died?"

His smile faded. "In a way. I had money in the bank and a nice place to live. I even persuaded her to visit me a few times in California. She was a stern old lady, but I respected her and what she'd done for me—taking me in like that."

"I heard that you haven't seen your parents since the day that they dropped you off at this house."

Morgan eased down beside her. His arm draped over her body, and he kissed her shoulder.

"That's true. I finally began to wonder if they were still alive, so Berk looked into it for me. He found my dad married again and living just outside Seattle." Morgan smiled. "He's what you'd call a tree hugger, but at least he's clean and sober. We don't have much to do with each other because he thinks I sold out to the almighty corporation. But we have talked."

"And your mother?"

He sighed. "Drugs ruined her life and finally fried her brain. She's in another rehab center upstate. Maybe it'll work this time."

Jane wanted to erase the sound of melancholy from his voice. She rolled over and kissed him.

"I think you gave me a hicky," she said, not caring even a little bit.

"That's not all I'm going to give you," Morgan said, pushing her onto her back.

"Promises, promises," Jane teased.

Someone pounding on the door roused Jane. She sat up in bed. Morgan was beside her, but he was dead to the world. She was a little stiff and more than a little sore. She and Morgan had tried to make up for ten years in one night.

Just as she became aware that dawn was peeking beneath the window shades, the pounding resumed. Morgan still didn't awaken.

Jane got out of bed and pulled the chenille spread from the floor and wrapped herself up in it. She padded barefoot to the door and peeked out the side of the curtain. In the dim light of dawn, she could see Berk and a strikingly beautiful young woman.

Uncertain as to what to do, she made her decision when Berk raised his fist and pounded on the door again.

Jane opened the door. "What is it?" she asked in a low voice.

She thought his eyes were going to pop out of his head. She clutched the spread tighter around her.

"Uh, is Morgan here?"

"Yes, but he's asleep."

"Oh." Berk fidgeted, shifting his weight from one foot to the other. "Well, can you wake him up? Or let me in and I'll wake him up."

"Can't it wait until later?" Jane eyed the young woman. Taller and absolutely beautiful, she looked familiar.

"*Oué*? What is going on here?" The woman stepped from behind Berk. "Get Morgan up at once," she ordered imperiously.

Jane's back went up. "Why don't you come back later?"

"Look. It was his idea for me to spend the weekend with him so go tell him I'm here."

"Serena, I think there's been a mistake," Berk said. "Why don't you go wait in the car?"

The woman winked at Jane. "Don't mind Berk. He's as fussy as an old lady. Morgan will want to know I'm here earlier than he expected me. He might be looking for a little action if you know what I mean."

"Yes. I think I do know what you mean," Jane said, her voice as calm as death.

"Perhaps I should go wake Morgan," Berk said, pushing open the door Jane held in a death grip.

Jane felt as if something inside her was dying a very painful death.

"Don't be silly, Berk. Just wait here. I'll be glad to do the honors," she said.

Her rage grew with every step she took as she covered the distance from the front door to the bedroom.

When she opened the bedroom door, Morgan finally stirred. His eyes opened. He greeted her with a lazy smile and held his arms wide. "Come here, sweetheart."

Jane knew that if she went near him she'd smack him so hard her hand would hurt. She gripped the spread and stalked over to where her dress lay. Her only safety—for herself and for him, the faithless, amoral, snake in the grass—was in keeping silent and getting out of there as fast as she could.

She grabbed the dress and shoes and bundled the lingerie and pantyhose together in a ball and stalked toward the doorway at the back of the bedroom.

"Jane, what's wrong?"

Luckily, the doorway led to a bathroom and not a closet.

"Nothing's wrong, sweetheart," she grated. Then all her rage erupted in the slamming of the door. It sounded as if a grenade went off. She could hear Morgan's roar of surprise, but she flipped the lock and ignored his immediate pounding on the door.

It only took her a second to get into her underwear and her dress. She tossed the hose into the trash basket and slid her feet into the ivory evening shoes. A glance in the mirror confirmed she looked worse than a fright.

With frenzied movements, she unlocked the door and threw it open. To her consternation, Morgan stood there without a stitch of clothing on.

"What is the matter with you this morning?" Morgan growled.

"Nothing. Nothing at all," Jane said, heading to the bedroom door as fast as her feet could take her.

"Nothing?" His voice got louder. He grabbed her arm. "Is this normally the way you act after a night of passion?"

His question was the fuse to the dynamite of her emotions. Jane whirled, wishing she could incinerate him on the spot with a lightning bolt of anger from her eyes.

"Passion?" she asked, forcing herself to be calm. "Is that what you call it? I just thought we were indulging in a little sex. You know the old saying. If you can't be with the one you love, love the one you're with."

Furious color flooded his face and other parts of his anatomy that she planned to forget—even if it took the rest of her life.

"What the hell is that supposed to mean?" he roared.

Jane laughed. It sounded brittle and harsh. "You're a bright boy. You figure it out. Now I've got to go. I forgot I had an early date this morning."

"A date? With whom."

"Uh-uh-uh! Just because I had sex with you doesn't give you any rights over me." Let him chew on that!

Jane opened the bedroom door. It took everything she had to say cheerfully, "Oh, Berk's here with your girlfriend. Should I send her back now or do you want to shower before you're ready for a little more action?"

Somehow, Jane got home without wrecking her mother's car, which was a miracle considering she was weeping enough to fill a bucket. She opened the kitchen door quietly, praying that her mom would be in the shower or asleep or something. She didn't know how she was going to explain staying out all night.

Unfortunately, luck seemed to have abandoned her

forever, Jane thought. Brenda Jones stood in the brightly lit kitchen pouring a cup of coffee.

She looked at Jane. Slowly. Up and down.

Jane cringed.

Brenda reached into the cupboard, pulled out another cup and filled it. She held it out. "Here, Janie."

Brokenly, Jane said, "Thanks, Mom." Then the tears came again.

Brenda encircled her with her arms and rocked her, making the same soothing sounds she had when Jane had been a child with a hurt. She never asked for an explanation.

"Go on upstairs, dear. You can miss church this morning. After your dad and I leave, come get some ice cubes for those eyes."

Brenda ruffled Jane's auburn curls. "Can't have you looking as if your heart is broken at the picnic this afternoon."

"Oh, Mom. I can't go to the picnic."

"I understand, dear. You don't care that everyone will know you're in hiding because Morgan Sherwood brought his Hollywood floozy here to flaunt her in front of you and the rest of the town."

A strangled half laugh escaped Jane. "How do you find these things out?"

"Well, Mr. Berkley stopped at the all-night convenience store to get a soda for Morgan's friend. Billy Tompkins was the clerk, and he recognized the young woman from some movie. Apparently, she and Morgan have been an item for quite some time."

Jane felt the tears flow again. "How did you know about Morgan?"

"I've always known, baby. Even in high school, I suspected."

"I'm sorry, Mom. I know I must be a disappointment."

"What utter nonsense. Jane, you are the pride of my life. You could never disappoint me." Brenda wiped her own eyes. "Now get upstairs before Dad gets up. You know how upset he gets about things."

Jane had to grin at that. Her dad was the calmest man she'd ever known. She suddenly realized that he balanced her mother very well.

"Thanks, Mom." She hugged her tightly. "I'll be ready to go to the picnic when you and Daddy get home from church."

Ten

Jane pulled her baseball cap down over her forehead. Makeup and sunglasses should take care of the rest of the ravages of her broken heart, she hoped, snapping the softball into the glove she wore on her left hand. The sun beat down unmercifully on her shoulders, left bare by the red tank top, and her legs, revealed in all their white-skinned glory by the cutoff jeans. There was no skin as white as a redhead's, she thought, disgruntled.

She could do this, Jane kept telling herself. She could play the dumb softball game, go to the barbeque, and even listen to the country band that was scheduled to play tonight. She'd even worn the dumb name tag in a gesture of defiance. She didn't quite know how she would manage to get through this ordeal, but somehow she would.

Morgan hadn't arrived yet. While her parents had been at church, the phone had rung so much she'd finally unplugged it. Once he wouldn't take her phone calls. Now she had the dubious pleasure of returning the disdain.

Brenda and Wes Jones sandwiched Jane, making her feel like a little girl again. She appreciated their support. Obviously, Brenda had said something to Wes because he kept calling her "baby doll" and kept a wary eye on anyone who approached.

"Dang! It's so hot birds are probably using potholders to pull worms out of the ground," Wes said.

Jane rewarded him with a weak smile. He chucked her under the chin.

The softball game was due to start in ten minutes. Jane had agreed to pitch when Amber, Jason, and the others had hounded her, refusing to take no for an answer. She just didn't have the energy to argue with them. She thought she could get through the afternoon and the barbeque tonight as long as she didn't have to look at Morgan and the beautiful Serena Maria Estevez.

Jane sighed. Then she saw Berk and Verna Wright arrive. Oh, no, she thought, steeling herself for the eventuality of seeing Morgan and Serena.

Amber ran up, dragging Steve with her. "Janie, what's going on? What's this about Morgan having a girlfriend?"

Jane tried to laugh, but stopped when it sounded so shaky. "Amber, you're behind on the gossip. You've got to start getting up earlier in the morning."

"It was all over church this morning. Some movie star rode into town in the limo bright and early."

"Oh, that," Jane said. "You must mean Serena Maria Estevez. That's quite a mouthful, isn't it?"

"Is she really that famous? Or is that just another exaggeration from the grapevine?"

"Oh, no. Everyone has seen her in the movies apparently. I'd say she looks like a young Natalie Wood—perhaps a bit more exotic."

"You ask me, that young man needs to get his head on straight," Wes grouched.

Brenda shushed Wes. "Oh, Janie, I think you should go warm up."

"Yes. I do need to flex the old pitching arm. Come on, Amber. You're umpire today."

"I am?" Amber asked. "Hey, I got promoted from outfield."

"Go get 'em, tiger," Steve said, patting her on the behind.

"Now, what's really going on?" Amber asked as she followed Jane to the diamond. So Jane told her an edited version of last night's events.

"Why, that lowdown, dirty, foul, son of a—"

"Shh. Speak of the devil," Jane muttered, feeling a sharp pain in the vicinity of her heart. "Here he comes."

Amber stood next to Jane, looking somewhat akin to a guard dog.

"Jane, I need to talk with you."

"Gee, sorry, Morgan. I've got a game to pitch." Jane walked toward the dugout.

"I tried to call you, but you didn't answer."

Jane couldn't resist. "Yeah. How'd that feel?" He stopped mid-stride but she kept going, knowing her knees would buckle if she stood still.

Morgan caught up with her. "Won't you let me explain?"

Jane stopped and turned. "No." Again, she

couldn't resist prodding him. "And how does that feel?"

She saw the anger in his eyes but he clamped down on whatever he was going to say.

Jane reached down and unpinned the name tag that had started her weekend of trouble. She tossed it to him. "Here, this served its purpose. I don't think I need it anymore since I've connected with all the single guys now."

Morgan looked as if he were going to throw it back in her face.

"Morgie. Morgie, over here."

Jane knew who that voice belonged to. She smiled snidely and said, "Your girlfriend is calling you, Morgie." She turned to the bleachers and saw the gorgeous brunette. The woman wore the tiniest hot pink minidress she'd ever seen. It was almost a misnomer to call it a dress. If she bent over, dozens of male eyes would probably explode from their sockets, judging by the attention being paid to the woman.

"This isn't over," Morgan warned, shoving the name tag in his pants pocket. Then he stalked away, leaving her standing alone on the baseball diamond.

"You're wrong," Jane said softly. "It was over ten years ago. I was just too stupid to know it."

Amber trotted up. "Bummer."

"Who cares about some actress?" Jane asked crossly. "I've never heard of her before."

"Steve said she was in the latest James Bond film." Amber shrugged. "We hardly ever go to the movies because of little Stevie. We just wait until they come out on video."

"She's taller than Morgan," Jane said, wanting to disparage the couple. "Taller than most of the men in fact."

"He doesn't look as if he cares," Amber said. Then she took one look at Jane's face. "I mean," she stammered, "they don't care."

Jane just didn't understand. How could he have made love to her so beautifully last night when he had asked this woman to meet him here today?

She was saved from further rumination when the rest of her team and the other team scrambled onto the field. To her horror, Morgan was pitcher for the other team. Great. That's all she needed, to have him out on the field and then facing her from the pitcher's mound.

By the fourth inning, Jane was physically whipped. She'd forgotten to apply sunscreen, and she could feel the wrath of a bad sunburn on every inch of uncovered skin. She suspected that she'd look quite a sight by tomorrow—assuming she didn't die of a broken heart first.

Morgan was at bat again. Jane took a deep breath, wound up, and threw a pitch that was way outside.

"Strike!" Amber called,

"What?" Morgan roared. He'd been struck out each time at bat, no matter how lousy a pitch Jane had thrown, though none of them had been quite as bad as the last one.

Her next pitch was way inside. He had to jump back to keep from being struck. Jane winced. She hadn't really meant to hit him. At least, she didn't think she had.

"Strike two!"

"You're crazy!" he yelled, not at Amber, but at Jane.

Jane waited while he scowled at her. When he was back in the batter's box, she let loose with her best fast ball. It hit the plate and ricocheted to the right.

"Strike three!" Amber yelled. "You're out!"

The people in the stands roared with laughter.

Morgan threw the bat down and stomped out to the pitcher's mound.

"You're going to listen to me if I have to gag you and tie you up," he snarled.

"Ooh. Sounds kinky," Jane drawled, pushing her sunglasses up on the bridge of her nose. "Maybe we can do it that way at our twentieth reunion."

He stood, fisted hands on hips. "I can definitely see why you never married. No man could put up with that irrational temper of yours."

Felicia ran up to Morgan and grabbed him. "Get back to the dugout, or you're gonna get thrown out of the game."

"I wouldn't want to give her the satisfaction," Morgan said, turning and going with Felicia.

Jane rolled her shoulders to relieve the tension. Would this game never end? Nothing like putting on a show for the hometown crowd, she thought cynically, scanning the faces in the stands.

She saw the beauteous Serena and Carlos in close conversation. The actress laughed, tossing her head back, and time itself seemed to have stood still the way every other man in the ball park turned to gaze at her.

Disgusting, Jane thought, winding up and throwing

the ball with all her might. Then she realized no one had taken the batter's box yet.

"Ow!" Verna shrieked, but she caught the ball and tossed it back. "Take it easy, Janie," she complained.

Eventually, the game ended with Morgan's team scoring one point more than her team.

Drooping, Jane headed for the covered picnic area. All she wanted was the biggest, coldest soft drink she could find.

"Good game, Janie," her dad said, handing her a thirty-two ounce cup full of ice water.

"Oh, thanks, Dad." She drained the cup halfway down then grabbed a handful of ice and swabbed it around her neck, shoulders, and chest.

"Oh, my goodness," Brenda breathed. "You're cooked."

"Yeah, I know. I forgot the sunscreen." Jane couldn't even feel the pain of the burn. She just felt its heat. "It'll be all right. A cool shower should tone down the red."

"Miss Jones, please wait."

It was Serena. Jane closed her eyes and counted to ten. She couldn't make a scene in front of her parents.

"I wanted to talk to you," Serena said.

Jane looked at her and hated her even more because she looked so cool and refreshed. By comparison, Jane knew she must look even worse.

"Yes, Miss Estevez, what can I do for you."

"Perhaps, we could speak later—alone?"

"Of course," she said, with automatic courtesy. "I just need a quick shower before the barbeque. If you'll excuse me until later?"

"Certainly," Serena said. "I'll go keep Morgan company. We'll save a seat for you at dinner."

"Yes, you do that, why don't you?" Jane snapped. When she realized how she'd sounded, she tacked on a smile.

"Come on, Janie," Brenda said. "I'll split some aloe vera leaves and coat you down good." She touched Jane's shoulder. "Maybe you should miss the rest of the events."

"No way. I'm not going to give him the satisfaction of thinking he hurt me."

"Who hurt you?" Wes asked, looking fierce.

"No one, Wes," Brenda said. "She's delusional from the heat."

Jane decided that the sun had fried her brain. That could be the only excuse for exposing herself to more hurt. She pulled up the pink tube top, feeling a bit underdressed, even with the soft white cotton tank over the tube top. Her skin was so tender that she hadn't been able to stand the thought of wearing anything more structured than the soft knit layers she'd pulled on. A pair of wide-legged white knit shorts and white sandals completed her ensemble.

She said a prayer of gratitude that storm clouds had kicked up a breeze and darkened the sky a little earlier than usual. The smell of barbeque and baked beans proved more nauseating than appealing to her weak stomach.

The band, with Amber's husband on drums and the

high school band director on steel guitar, had already warmed up and was playing a Garth Brooks song.

"Oh, my goodness," Amber cried when Jane sat next to her on the long bench. "You look like a reverse raccoon."

"Thanks loads. That's just what I needed to bolster my spirits," Jane said, tentatively touching her face—red everywhere except where the sunglasses and the brim of the ball cap had shielded her.

"Where's your mom and dad?" Amber asked.

"They decided to stay home in the air-conditioning."

Jane looked at the crowd under the pavilion. Most of the town seemed to have turned out for the party tonight. Strands of tiny white lights criss-crossed the rafters, providing just enough light to be able to see but not enough to see well.

Jane closed her tired eyes and leaned her forehead on the picnic table. "I wish I'd stayed home with Mom and Dad." Only four more hours and she could finally make her escape.

"Janie, are you asleep?"

"Verna?" Jane opened one eye. "No, I'm just resting my eyes."

Verna Wright looked at her with such concern in her dark eyes that Jane asked, "What's wrong, Verna?"

"Oh, Janie, I don't know what to do." Verna wrung her hands in dismay.

"What are you talking about?"

"I know I shouldn't but I can't stand the thought of you getting hurt. You don't deserve it. Even if you did start this."

"Start what? Would you come to the point, I'm too tired to play guessing games."

"Don't sleep with Morgan," Verna blurted out.

"I don't think that's any of your business."

"Well, it is. I heard Morgan talking to Berk. Berk's a dear, Janie. I heard him tell Morgan that what he planned to do wasn't right. Berk tried to talk him out of it."

"What are you talking about?"

"Morgan overheard you and Amber talking about him. He heard you plan to seduce him and then toss him away—like an old shoe, he said."

Jane stared at Verna. Morgan had overheard that stupid conversation? And he believed she was serious?

"He's planning on doing it to you first."

"Doing what to me first?" Jane straightened, unable to believe what she was hearing.

Even when Verna explained in detail, she couldn't believe he had deliberately seduced her, just to humiliate her with his—his actress bimbo.

"You mean this has all been an act? Some kind of get-me-before-I-get-him payback? Verna, I was joking. Amber and I were just being silly. If Morgan heard that, then he didn't hear what went before."

Jane looked at the two women. "Morgan made love with me just so he could drop me? Because he thought I was going to do that to him?"

Verna looked stricken. "I knew I should have told you before now. I'm so sorry."

Jane was stunned. Though she'd been hurting before, she hadn't realized the full impact of what had happened. She felt as if her heart was going to break. She couldn't breathe.

"Sit down," Verna commanded.

"Put your head between your knees," Amber ordered.

"No, no. I'm okay." Jane laughed, but it choked and turned into a sob. "I just realized I've fallen in love with Morgan—all over again. And it's just as hopeless now as it was then."

He had never been in love with her at all. How could she have been so wrong about him? For a moment, she thought she was going to throw up.

"I'll be right back." Amber dashed away and was back in a couple of minutes with a stack of paper towels and some ice. "Here, Janie." She pressed the wet towels against the back of Jane's neck. "Take deep breaths."

She heard footsteps. *Please don't let it be him,* she begged silently.

Apparently, her prayer wasn't going to be answered.

"What's wrong with Jane?" Morgan asked. She felt him kneel in front of her.

She opened her eyes and looked into his.

He winced. "You look like a broiled lobster."

"Thank you for noticing," Jane said, straightening. "Was there something you needed, Morgan? Something else, that is?" she asked in a nasty voice.

He flushed. "I think there's something we need to talk about." He stood.

Wasn't he satisfied yet? Or did he have to tell her face-to-face to kiss off? She wasn't about to let him have that satisfaction.

"Well, I'm supposed to dance with Jason right now. So maybe I can fit you in afterward—if I don't duck out with Jason, that is."

She flounced away, trying her best to shake her hips and look as if she knew where she was going.

Luckily, she spied Jason and Felicia talking over by the dessert table.

"Jason, let's dance," she said, pasting a grin on her face.

"Oh, Janie, uh." He looked undecided. His eyes bounced from Felicia to Jane.

"Oh, I'm sorry," Jane said. "I interrupted something, didn't I?"

"No, not at all," Jason said, leaving Felicia holding two plates of peach cobbler.

Over his shoulder, Jane saw Felicia scowl and slam the two plates down.

"I did interrupt something. I'm so sorry."

"Hey, no problem. She's so desperate, it won't matter."

His comment absolutely floored Jane. What a jerk. If she wasn't so intent on proving to Morgan that he meant nothing to her, she'd have told Jason what she thought about him.

As it was, she went stiffly into his arms and danced the two-step even though brushing against him hurt her reddened skin.

When the song ended, Jane thanked him and moved to another boy from her high school class whom she knew was single. Though the rest of the evening dragged on leaden feet, she played the part of belle of the ball. She danced until she thought her feet would fall off.

After she'd turned Morgan down three times, always graciously and with a wide smile, he didn't ask her anymore but his eyes never left her. Jane made sure to flirt with every guy she saw and danced with anyone who asked her. Her heart felt as if it were bleeding. The heat of the evening began to dissipate with the storm clouds that finally unleashed a little of the rain they held. The moisture felt good on her baked skin.

The band under the pavilion kept on playing and nearly everyone kept dancing. Jane sat one out, deciding to refresh herself with a cold drink.

When Jason finished dancing with Felicia, he approached her. By this time of night, he looked as if he'd had something a bit stronger than soda. Someone must have smuggled a bottle in.

"Come on, Janie. Let's dance."

A slow love song, a new arrangement of a Patsy Cline hit, was being played. Jane went into his arms. When they swayed, hardly without moving, she saw Morgan shake his head and turn to leave. Serena, Carlos, and Penny followed.

It was over. At last, she thought, shoulders slumping tiredly.

The dance became a tug of war with Jason trying to grind his pelvis into her abdomen. She was repelled. She didn't want to know he wanted her. Though she suspected he just chased any woman.

"So tell me, Jason, how has life treated you?" she asked, moving away from him.

She listened while he told of making partner in his law firm just two years ago. He talked about his new Porsche, his condo on the river front, and his planned vacation in Aspen.

At no time did he mention his failed marriage or the child Jane had heard about.

"I heard you had a daughter."

"Oh, yeah. She's two."

"Do you see her often?"

He squirmed. "Actually, no. What does a guy like me do with a toddler?"

His apathetic attitude incensed her. "Maybe be a father to her. After all, you helped bring her into the world," she said, censure in her tone.

He looked at her oddly. "I thought a feminist like you would have a more modern attitude about children."

Jane stiffened. "Every feminist I know is dedicated to making the world a better place for children. Being a feminist doesn't mean being anti-children. It means guaranteeing equal pay for equal work and concepts like that. It means giving women the right to stay home and feel good about themselves, or to work and feel good about themselves. Those options aren't mutually exclusive."

"You're not nearly as much fun as you used to be, Janie. You're far too serious. Even in high school, you had some kind of moral code that kept your legs locked at the knee."

Jane froze. "Jason, I used to think you were my friend. I remember how you rescued me and took me to the prom when my plans fell apart. But all you were interested in was getting in my pants. Then and now, I assume."

He shrugged cockily. "Well, I thought since you hadn't married that you might be fun this weekend. Plus, I knew old Morgan would be here sniffing around your skirts like a hound after a bitch in heat. I thought it might be fun to see if I could snow him again like in high school."

"What do you mean by that? And how do you know about Morgan?"

"We were buds in high school. Or he thought we were. Can't figure out how a guy like him became so successful when he's so gullible."

"What did you do to Morgan in high school?"

"Not much. Told him you were using him to improve your calculus grade. That you had no interest in him otherwise. Poor schmuck. He thought you were actually in love with him, and he bought it—lock, stock, and barrel. The truth just broke his nerdy heart. Unbelievable."

So that was why Morgan had coldly ignored her those last days of high school. Jason had convinced him that she was using him. Jane realized why it had been so easy for Morgan to believe she planned to seduce him this weekend, then toss him away. He thought she'd done the same thing ten years ago. Suddenly, a lot of things—like Serena, some of Penny's comments, the things Morgan had said—made sense.

"I don't know any words foul enough to call you, even though I've lived in New York for ten years where profanity is practically an art form." Jane shoved him away. "Don't cross my path again. You won't like what I do to you."

"Are you threatening me?" Jason asked incredulously.

"No, I'm promising you."

Jane walked off, leaving him alone on the dance floor. She looked around for Morgan but he wasn't there. He'd been wrong to try to hurt her, yet she understood now why he'd done it. They might not have a future together, but she owed him an explanation for the past.

It was nearly midnight. Would he still be in town? She had to find him and tell him the truth. He must know the truth.

She found Amber and told her she was leaving. Then she ran to her mom's car and took off. On a whim, she drove to the Dairy Palace first, but there was no car parked behind it.

Jane wasted no time in getting over to his grandmother's house. Her heart felt a pang of regret as she thought about the beautiful night that had ended so tragically. It was as much her fault as his.

To her shock, the limo was gone. And so was the little Toyota he'd driven last night.

Jane parked and climbed the steps. The front door was locked. No matter how hard she pounded on the door, no one answered.

Morgan was gone.

Eleven

She'd lost him.

That thought hit Jane with the force of a sledge-hammer and nearly brought her to her knees. She sank onto the top step. Her head fell into her hands. She wanted to weep, but she didn't think she had any tears left after last night.

"No!" she cried, refusing to accept defeat. She shouted it again. The word rang out into the night.

Jane leaped up. "I won't let him go." She'd lost him once before when he'd stolen away like a thief in the night. She wouldn't let him do it again. She owed him an explanation, and he owed her an apology. After that, she'd see if there was anything worthwhile between them.

Jane dashed to the Chevy. She wasn't a kid now. She knew how to stop him this time.

The tires squealed on the pavement when she whipped into the driveway at her parents' home and parked beside her dad's cruiser. Jane dashed through the back door and up the stairs, takings them two at a time.

"Dad! Daddy, wake up," she called, running into her parents' bedroom.

"Wha?" her dad said groggily. "Janie, what's going on? Did the station call?" Wes Jones raised up, bleary-eyed from having awakened from a deep sleep.

"No, Dad. I need you to do something for me. I promise I'll never ask for another favor as long as I live if you'll just do this one little thing for me."

He sighed. "What's wrong, Janie?"

"It's Morgan. He's left town. I want you to stop him," she blurted out.

"Stop him? Why? Did he break a law? Steal something?" he whispered, glancing over at her mother.

"Yes. Yes, Daddy, he stole something."

"What did he steal?"

"My heart."

Her father looked at her clearly then. "Janie, I can't go around arresting a guy just because he broke your heart—even if I'd like to."

"Dad, you've got to stop him. You're the sheriff. Can't you put up a roadblock or put out an all-points bulletin or something?"

"Have you completely lost your mind?" he whispered. "Go to bed. You'll wake your mother."

"I'm already awake," Brenda said, pushing herself up against the headboard.

"Please, Dad. This is important. It's the most important thing I've ever asked before."

Brenda studied her daughter. She reached out and pulled Jane down to sit on the bed. "Can't you call him, honey?"

"No. He won't ever talk to me again if he gets away. I understand that now."

Her eyes beseeched her father for support and understanding.

"Do it, Wes," Brenda said softly.

"What? I can't abuse the power of my office just because my daughter has some kind of romantic problem."

"Jane's right. You're the only one who can help her now. Stop Morgan from getting away."

"Oh, Dad, please. Don't you remember how you told me you let Mom go when you arrested her at that protest? You did that because you were attracted to her. If you hadn't, you'd never have gotten to know her and I wouldn't be standing here asking you to think with your heart instead of your head."

Wes sighed. "Why couldn't I have had sons instead of daughters?"

Brenda smiled. "Wait downstairs for your father, Janie. He'll be right down."

Jane paced in the kitchen. It felt like hours had passed since she'd been at Morgan's house, but in reality, less than an hour had crept by on the clock.

When her dad walked into the kitchen, he was dressed in his khaki uniform. "Let's go," he said.

Jane squealed and hugged him. "Hurry. He has nearly an hour head start."

Wes backed out of the driveway and reached for his cell phone instead of the police radio. He called the station and spoke to the deputy on duty.

"No, I don't want this out over the air waves, Buddy, but I do want that limo stopped."

He spoke for a while longer, giving instructions on how he wanted them to proceed.

"Okay, Janie, now we go to the station and wait."

* * *

"Which one of you lifted the silver?" Berk asked, slowing.

"What do you mean?" Penny asked. Morgan remained silent, staring out the window at the darkness.

"I mean there's a police cruiser with lights flashing coming up behind us."

"Keep going," Penny said. "They couldn't be after us. They're probably looking for moonshiners or something."

Berk laughed. "Penny, you know even less about the police than you do about modern southern culture."

"All I know is that these southern guys can dance your feet off," she complained, massaging her bare feet.

Berk slowed and let the police cruiser pass. When it slowed in front of him and angled to the shoulder of the road, he obligingly pulled over.

"What's going on?" Morgan asked rousing from his misery.

"I know I wasn't speeding," Berk said. "You tell me. You're the one involved with the sheriff's daughter."

"Don't be ridiculous," Morgan snapped.

Berk rolled the window down when the officer approached.

"Can you step out of the car, sir," the officer politely asked.

"Sure, deputy." Berk opened the door and stepped out onto the pavement.

The deputy next asked for his license, proof of insurance, proof of registration or rental agreement. When he seemed to be taking an inordinate amount of time to study the documents, Morgan's temper hit the boiling point.

Morgan climbed out of the car. "This is harassment," he complained. "Plain and simple. I'm going to call my lawyer about this if you detain us one minute more."

The deputy looked at him calmly. "Just one minute, sir." He walked back to his cruiser.

They could see him using a cellular phone. "That guy doesn't look old enough to drive," Morgan pointed out, "much less be an officer of the law."

Carlos and Serena climbed out of the car. Serena stretched gracefully. "Is this more of the southern fun?" She leaned against Carlos who gladly supported her and wrapped his arms around her.

The kid looked like a puppy as he gazed adoringly at the young woman. Morgan was surprised by how quickly they had taken to each other. It had been love at first sight, he supposed, feeling a shade bitter at the thought.

"Is this going to take all night?" Penny asked, from the car door.

"It may. Put your shoes on and get a breath of fresh air," Berk said.

"Fresh air? There's no such thing in this state. It's still ninety-five degrees out here."

"Ninety-five? Hey, that's almost chilly," Berk said with a grin.

"How do they live here in this heat, day in and day out?" Penny grumbled.

"You didn't seem to have much difficulty with the heat when you were acting like Cinderella at the ball." Berk grinned.

The deputy walked back just then. "Oh, Penny." He doffed his western style hat. "I didn't think I'd see you again so soon."

"Why, Clyde. What are you doing here?"

He scuffed the pavement with the toe of his boot. "Actually, I'm arresting you and the others."

"What?" squawked five voices in unison.

"Sorry, folks, but the sheriff has ordered me to bring you all in."

"This is an outrage," Morgan said with cold fury. "I demand you let us continue on our way."

"Now, Mr. Sherwood, I can't do that. And if you don't settle down, I'll have to charge you with resisting arrest too."

Everyone started talking at that. A babble of voices rose at that. In the distance, Morgan could hear the wailing of a siren. They turned and watched another cruiser approach. It screeched to a halt and two more deputies climbed out.

"Okay, folks, you can do this the easy way or the hard way," an older deputy barked.

Within minutes, the limo had been turned and was being driven back to town by one of the deputies.

Clyde, the first deputy on the scene, had Penny in the front seat next to him and Morgan and Berk locked behind the grill in the backseat.

"You seem to be awfully amused by this," Morgan said sourly to Berk.

"Hey, this is probably something I'll be telling my grandchildren about." Berk laughed loudly.

The other deputy, with Carlos and Serena in the backseat, followed in the second cruiser.

Morgan cursed all the way back. He was so angry he wanted to throttle Jane Jones. He knew this was her doing. She obviously hadn't humiliated him enough. What else had she planned? Maybe she had called the tabloids with this scoop.

He wouldn't be surprised to see camcorders and strobe lights when he got to the jail. But when they pulled up to the parish courthouse, there was no mob out front. Only a few lights were on in the hallway that led to the sheriff's office and the jail.

When he walked in, he saw the sunburned cause of his current predicament.

"You!" he accused. He walked over and jabbed his index finger into the air in front of her face. "When I get finished with you, you'll be lucky if someone hires you to design toilet paper."

"Now, Morgan," Jane said, striving for a calm she didn't feel. "I just wanted to talk to you."

"Why? Wasn't our one-night stand enough for you?"

"What?" Wes Jones roared.

Morgan's head snapped around. He'd forgotten they had an audience.

"Throw that son of a"—Wes remembered his daughter—"gun in the cell," he ordered.

Clyde took Morgan by the arm. "This way, Mr. Sherwood. You've gone and done it now."

"You've just bought yourself a big fat lawsuit, Sheriff Jones," Morgan said. He went, willingly but stiffly.

The chatter from Morgan's friends increased in volume.

"Daddy. Let me talk to him."

"If there's any talking to do, you can talk to me, little lady," he said, sounding as stern as he looked.

Jane rolled her eyes. "Daddy, I'm nearly thirty years old! Quit treating me as if I'm your virgin daughter."

Wes turned red to the tip of his ears. "Why couldn't I have had sons?" he muttered, raising his eyes to the ceiling.

Jane grinned. "It's okay, Dad. Maybe you'll have grandsons."

"You and your sisters are responsible for every one of these gray hairs. And you're the sensible one of the bunch."

"I know, Daddy, and I'm sorry." Jane tried to sound as contrite as possible.

Wes sighed. "Don't try to sweet talk me. Save that for Morgan. I have a feeling you're going to need every bit of charm you got just to get him to listen to you."

Clyde came back into the room. "What do you want to do with the rest of these people, Sheriff?"

Wes rubbed both hands over his face. "Let 'em sit out here until we get this sorted out. Just don't let them make any phone calls, or I may be looking for a new job in the morning."

"Right, Sheriff," Clyde said.

"Make some coffee and send over to the diner for some peach pie. Maybe that'll appease them until they can leave," Wes said.

"Okay, little girl. It's your show. You've got fifteen minutes with my prisoner."

Jane went through the big iron door that separated the jail from the offices. Morgan paced the cell they'd placed him in. He looked as mean as a caged tiger with a sore paw.

When he glanced up and saw her, he halted. "I bet you didn't come to give me my phone call, did you?"

Jane shook her head. Now that she had him as a captive audience, she found herself at a loss for words. There was so much she wanted to say—and needed to say.

He shrugged as if he didn't care. "Hey, no problem. I'm going to sue you, and this whole town." His grin held little humor. "And especially you, you fruitcake."

"Morgan, it's the only way I could think of to get you to talk to me. I apologize for these storm trooper tactics, but I was desperate. I knew that once you left town, I'd never be able to get to you."

"I don't think we have anything to talk about, Miss Jones," he said. If his expression hadn't warned her that he'd shut her out, his voice clearly did. "Talk to you? I tried all day and all night to talk to you. Well, I don't want to talk to you anymore. I don't ever want to see you again or hear your name. If I see you coming, I'll cross the street to avoid you."

"Just listen, please. I want to tell you a story," Jane said softly, moving to a position directly in front of him.

"What is this? Some kinky benefit for the prisoners in this parish? You come in and tell bedtime stories?"

"When I finish," Jane said, unperturbed by his sarcasm, "if you still want to leave, then you'll be free to go."

"Great. Get on with it. I want out of this nutty town."

"The only requirement is that you look at me when I talk." Jane waited. Then his eyes met hers. She saw such raw pain in their depths—just for an instant—that she knew she'd done the right thing. She had to make things right with him, even if he chose to leave afterward.

"Once upon a time—ten years ago, to be precise—a silly high school girl fell in love with the school genius. They were a funny, mismatched couple, and she didn't realize that he was a sensitive soul who thought she was ashamed of him. She didn't know that's why he never asked her for a date—that he was afraid she'd turn him down rather than be seen with him in public. She only knew there was something about him that made her heart beat faster. Inexperienced as she was, she didn't know that he was her soul mate."

"What a crock," Morgan blustered, turning away.

"You agreed to listen and look at me," she said, hating the tears that rose as she went on.

"She thought they would always be together. Imagine her shock when he suddenly told her to get lost. When he wouldn't talk to her at school or answer her phone calls." Jane blinked back the tears.

"Then imagine her shock when she learns that a boy she'd thought was her friend had orchestrated that cold rejection."

"What are you trying to say?" Morgan asked, tense and strained.

"I'm saying that Jason lied to you. Just as you later

decided for yourself. I'm saying that when you overheard Amber and me, I was joking to hide the hurt I
still felt at your rejection. I never had any intention of
seducing you and then dropping you."

Morgan frowned. "Say what you've got to say in
plain English."

"Okay. I'll be bluntly honest. If you think back over
the last few days, you'll realize that you made every
move. I merely responded to you."

Jane grasped the bars and pulled herself close. "Oh,
Morgan. I'm trying to say I loved you ten years ago,
and I still love you."

Jane pushed the iron door open and stepped into
the office. She felt a heady combination of tiredness
and exhilaration.

Carlos sat in one of the desk chairs with Serena
curled into his lap. Her arms encircled his neck. They
looked up at her.

Penny, who seemed to be illustrating the finer
points of some dance step to Clyde, paused and looked
over at Jane.

Berk stopped in mid-motion, halting what appeared
to be a martial arts movement he was demonstrating
to her father, and looked at her.

Wes Jones raised both eyebrows in question.

Nearly in unison, everyone in the room asked,
"Everything all right?"

Laughter bubbled out of Jane. "Everything is fine."
She launched herself at her father and hugged him
until he was laughing too.

"Sheriff," she said, grinning, "would you mind releasing your prisoner into my custody?"

"I don't know. He seems like a right violent sort of fellow. You sure you can handle him?"

Jane grinned with happiness. "Piece of cake, Dad."

Twelve

"I knew Jason wanted you, yet I still believed him when he told me you were using me." Morgan teased the soft curls that brushed against her forehead.

"I can't believe a man with your intelligence couldn't see through him." Jane snuggled against his side, determined to let him know for every day of the rest of their lives together how very much she loved him.

"Hey, I was desperately in love with a girl I thought was unattainable. And I didn't have a great track record of people staying with me."

His shrug was a sensual motion as the bare skin of his shoulder pressed sweetly against her face. She dropped a kiss on his collarbone.

"What can I say? Insecurity does funny things to people. I didn't realize how much it still drove me."

"Well, maybe a little love and attention will finally get rid of it." Jane's leg slid over his. She relished the hair-roughened muscles.

"I'd say so," Morgan said, easing over her body.

"Not again?" Jane said in mock complaint.

"Hey, give a guy a break. I've got years of unrequited love to make up for."

Jane threw the covers aside. "Then what are you waiting for?"

His kiss silenced her laughter.

When the sensual storm was over, Jane drifted off to sleep with a lingering look of love on her face.

At eight o'clock the next morning, she wasn't smiling as she dressed.

"What are we going to tell my parents?" she asked, pausing to watch Morgan.

He wasn't doing anything extraordinary, just buttoning his white shirt. Then he stuffed the shirttail into a pair of jeans. It was unnerving how excited he made her as she watched him in the simply act of dressing.

"Caught you looking," he said, smiling.

She turned her attention to her own clothes. Her sunburn felt rather worse for the activity of the evening.

"My parents? How do we explain last night?" she asked again.

"I don't think we need to draw them a picture," Morgan said with a wink. He reached into his pocket. "Oh, by the way, I have something for you." He handed her the name tag that had kicked off her reunion with a bang. It no longer read Jane-I'm-Still-Single-Jones. He'd crossed out the middle words.

Jane read aloud, "Jane-I'm-Very-Married-Jones." She didn't think she could be happier, but she'd been wrong.

She made a mock frown. "No, I won't wear that."

"Why not?" He looked taken aback.

She reached for the pen in his shirt pocket and wrote on the name tag, then held it up.

"I won't wear it unless you add the name Sherwood."

He read, "Jane-I'm-Very-Married Jones-Sherwood." Morgan grinned. "I can live with that."

"Do you really mean it?" she asked, unable to maintain her blasé attitude.

"Let's tell your folks we're getting married as soon as that sunburn peels off." He leaned over and kissed her softly. "I want you to look fabulous in your wedding dress."

Jane felt as if she were floating on a cloud as Morgan drove to her parents' home. Everything had worked out more perfectly than she'd imagined in her wildest dreams.

When he turned onto her street, she saw cars lining both sides of the street. The tail fins of Miss Mamie's big blue Cadillac jutted out into the street like a beached whale.

"Oh, dear," she said, jumping out of the car. "I hope nothing has happened."

When she and Morgan walked into the house, silence greeted them. Jane hoped her sunburn obscured her rising blush.

Gathered around the dining table were her parents, her grandmother, Amber, Morgan's friends, and nearly all the members of the Vernon Ladies Bridge Club.

"What's going on here?" she asked, looking at her mother.

Brenda shook her head. "Sorry, Janie. Privacy is what you give up in exchange for people who care about you, I guess. It's the curse—and the blessing—of small town life."

"We heard about the wedding and wanted to come congratulate you and Morgan," Mamie Holt said.

"Maybe my bed is bugged," Morgan whispered in her ear.

"Shhh," Jane said. Her exasperation warred with amusement at the thought of the small town's gossip mill.

"Are there going to be any more movie stars at the wedding? I just love that Leonardo boy who was in *Titanic*," Mamie continued, fluttering her false eyelashes. "Or maybe you know that gentleman from Australia? Mel Gibson? He's really got the cutest tushie I've ever seen." Mamie blushed and laughed like a young girl.

Amusement won. Jane laughed, and Morgan joined in.

"Miss Mamie," he said, "for you, I'll see if I can get one of them here for the wedding."

Morgan and Jane smiled and gladly received everyone's good wishes. As soon as they could slip away, they escaped to the back porch.

She smiled up at him with her heart in her eyes. "So what happens now?"

"Remember that story you were telling me in the jail?"

Puzzled, Jane nodded.

"It began 'once upon a time' so it's only logical that it end in the classic way."

"You mean?"

"Yes," he said, brushing a kiss onto her lips, "now we live happily ever after."

ABOUT THE AUTHOR

Joan Reeves has a husband who thinks she hung the moon, four children who think they are adults, and a dog who thinks she's a person—all the ingredients for a life warmed by laughter. She thinks that love is the greatest of all the riches and that laughter smooths the rough edges of life.

She loves to hear from readers and invites you to write her (please send SASE for a personal reply and an autographed bookplate) at P. 0. Box 680568, Houston TX 77268-0568 or e-mail:

reeves-writes-novels@juno.com.